I0775445

HENGIST

Sean Poage

Apeiron Press LLC

443 Western Avenue #1005
South Portland, Maine 04106

Hengist
Copyright © 2023, Sean Poage

First Apeiron Press Trade Edition, November 2023
First Apeiron Press Ebook Edition, November 2023

Cover design: Dmitry Yakhovsky
© Sean Poage, 2023
Map art: Sean Poage
© Sean Poage, 2023

Apeiron Press Trade Paperback: ISBN-13:
979-8-9886101-0-6
Apeiron Press eBook Edition: ISBN-13:
979-8-9886101-1-3

Published in the United States of America

Contents

Dedicated to Ruth Heusinkveld, my high school librarian, and all the teachers who had to put up with my antics, knowing I could do better. All their work was not in vain.

In 1987, Mrs. Heusinkveld put a book in my hand that would one day inspire me to become a published author.

HENGIST

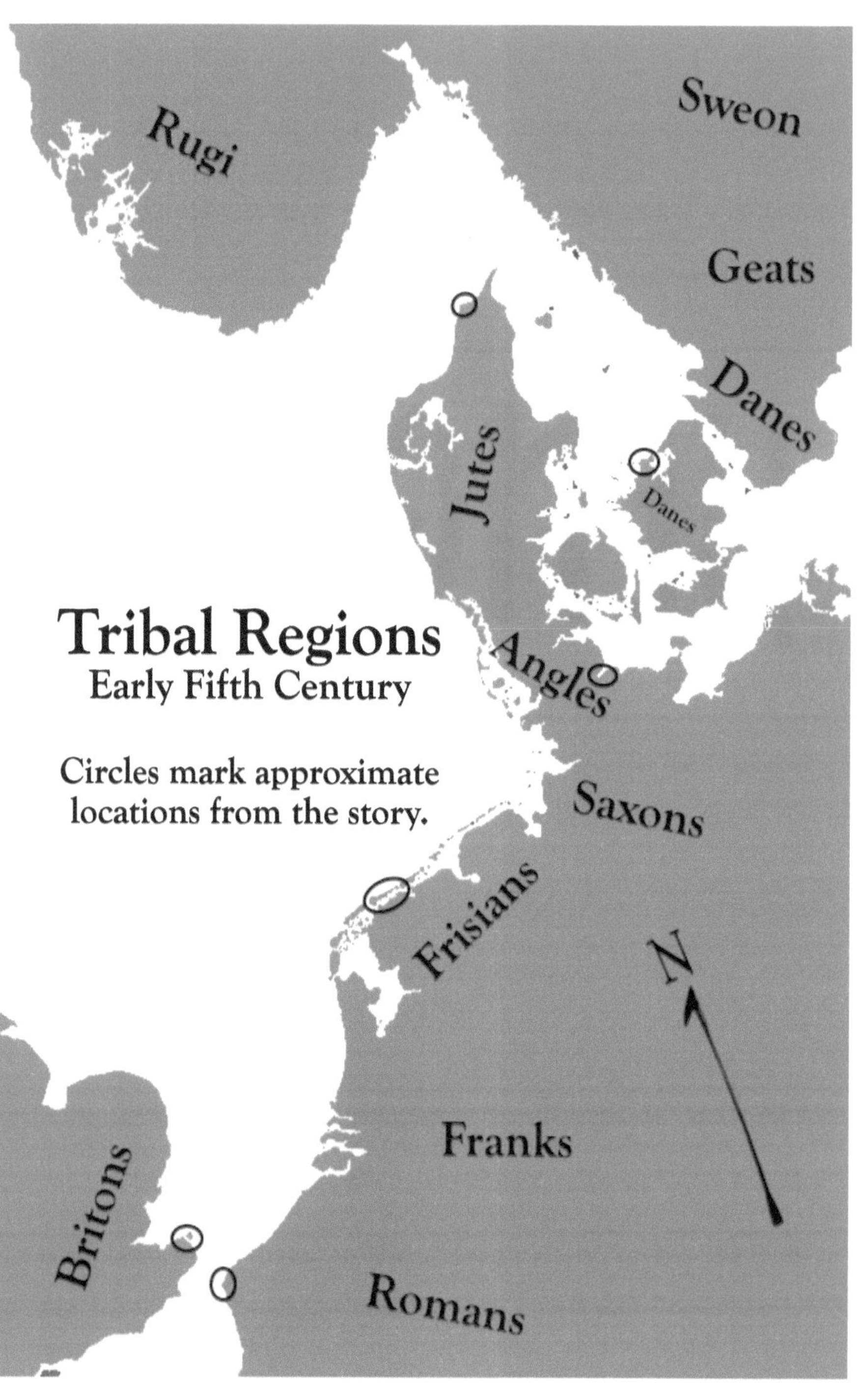

Rugi
Sweon
Geats
Danes
Jutes
Danes
Angles
Tribal Regions
Early Fifth Century
Circles mark approximate
locations from the story.
Saxons
Frisians
N
Franks
Britons
Romans

I

A Ring-Prowed Ship

427 A.D.

An old witch once called me a plaything of the Fates. It explains my fortunes: rising, falling, and rising again, like waves upon the sea. The witch said their game ends with my name either lost to time, or never forgotten. I intend the latter. My name is Hengist, son of Wihtgils, son of Witta, in direct descent from Woden All-Father.

In my twelfth summer, my father fell gloriously in battle. My brother, born of my father's first wife and the elder by twelve years, drove me from my home the day I reached manhood. He feared a lad of fifteen winters might wrest away his primogeniture. He did not even have the courage to kill me outright. Far simpler, he thought, to let the sea do it. No blood upon his cowardly hands. So, he sent me away with a skeleton crew of old men and timid slaves, and no more wealth than our spears and my ship.

It was a relief, truly, to be cut adrift.

I did not fear. My father taught me to sail by making me build this ring-prowed ship. I know her so intimately I could sail her over a waterfall. When my father gave me this vessel, he gave me my life.

That life was difficult, eked out with piracy, sometimes trading or, when the Fates were particularly malicious, in fishing. Yet I made a name for myself, through skill, bravery, and generosity. Stout warriors joined my crew. A score have gone to Woden's halls over the years, but not one has left me willingly.

Twenty-seven make up my warband now. Mostly house-less Jutes, like Eaha, some Anglii like me, and a few Saxons, like Sigeferth. All doughty, deadly, and loyal to the last. Four summers ago, I put my sword and my ship in the service of Hoc, a king of Danes in the Juteland. He was good to me, and we distinguished ourselves in his wars in the Juteland, Scandia, and all along the East Sea.

Hoc died this past spring. He was nearly a father to me. I would have taken my warband and sailed in search of new adventures and lands of our own, but his son, Hnæf, showered me with gifts and convinced me to stay in his service. A few years younger than I, Hnæf has much of his father in him.

He showed me greater honour by requesting my ship for a journey to visit his sister, Hildeburh, wife of the Frisian king, Finn Folcwalding. Per custom, Hoc had fostered their son, Frithuwulf, and Hnæf had mentored the boy. Now a man, it was time for Frithuwulf to return to his father's hall.

Hoc's death, his funeral, and Hnæf's duties in ascending the throne delayed that return. We finally set out in the last days of the sailing season, which meant wintering at Finns-burg. I could think of few better ways to pass the ice-months than feasting at the table of the wealthiest king in Frisia.

We neared Finn's coast, pushed by an icy wind that boded a bitter winter. My ship was laden with me and my men, Frithuwulf, Hnæf, and thirty of his own household war-riors.

I craned to find my mark, a dark split in the grassy mud-flats, and leaned on the steering board to bring the course to bear. Eaha waited for my nod, then gave the order to drop the sail. The ropes creaked, and the mast groaned as the boom scraped against it on the way down.

A rogue wave rose and dropped suddenly, causing the hull to slam against the water. A man lost his grip on the spray-slimed rope, and the sail fell with a flapping thud, spraying salty water across everyone, raising a chorus of curses. Abruptly released from the driving wind, the long, sleek vessel heeled over, then righted and shuddered to a stop as the prow rose on a swell.

"Grip the rope like a man, Eadwig!" Eaha barked. "The rest of you stop complaining, stow the sail and get on the oars."

Eaha blustered for the Danes' sake—my men were all well drilled. In short order, they wrapped the sail, turned the boom and lashed it to the deck-trees. The men set the oars and pulled for the grey-green shore. I steered towards a gap in the reeds that would take us through the salt marshes and on to our destination.

A scuffling and groan from behind told me that the commotion had roused Hnæf from his doze. He crawled out from under the leather tarp lashed between the gunnels and stretched, yawning loudly.

"Ah, now, we're nearly there, eh?"

"Your man said Finnsburg is through that channel." I lifted my chin to the east. "We'd doubtless see hearth smoke if not for this wind."

Hnæf nodded and called out to a gangling youth sitting by the mast, practising knot tying with one of my sailors. "Frithuwulf!" He waved the boy over.

Frithuwulf stood and picked his way past the rowers to join us. "Yes, Uncle?"

"So, there are the lands of your birth." Hnæf swept his hand out to the shore, smiling. "It must be good to see them again."

The boy looked at the thick, green grasses and narrow, sandy beaches stretching north and south. The landscape was utterly flat and treeless. "It was so long ago." He frowned and shifted uncomfortably. "I've spent more of my life in your home than . . . mine."

Hnæf nodded and squeezed Frithuwulf's shoulder. "Your father and mother will be pleased to have you back, but you'll always have a home in our hall. And you will always be my brother."

Watching Frithuwulf beam at Hnæf, I suppressed a feeling of bitterness for the experience I had from my own brother.

We crossed the surge and rowed into the marshes, weaving between muddy shoals and grassy islets. Before long, the gold-thatched rooves of Finnsburg came to view. The salty wind brought the scent of cow dung and peat fires, and the bleat of sheep and lowing of cattle.

The settlement stood upon an island, expanded and raised above the seasonal floodmark by generations of human labour. Most of the houses were of sod or wattle-and-daub. Only a few were of whitewashed timber, including the great hall. It stood on a mound that elevated it above the other buildings. Someone in the burg sounded a bell, announcing our approach.

Ordlaf, Hnæf's kinsman and captain, lifted his horn and blew the peace-hail. Steel glinted as soldiers came out of the great hall and moved towards the shore, ready to defend against hostile visitors. When we rowed to within hailing distance and they learnt who had arrived, a cheer erupted.

By the time we reached the docks, an enthusiastic crowd had gathered: soldiers, fishermen, children, women. Shouts behind them made the throng split, and the old king strode to the wharf, Hildeburh on his arm and his personal guard following.

Hnæf and Frithuwulf went ashore, followed by his Danes. While they enjoyed a warm welcome from Finn and his queen, my men and I secured the ship and unpacked the gifts Hnæf had brought: furs, soapstone, iron bars, and amber. Then we waited. Let the Danes have their reception, but we were not their labourers.

Guthlaf, Ordlaf's brother, finally noticed us sitting back by the goods and, embarrassed, sent men to collect them. Finn then led us all on a merry tromp through his burg to the meadhall.

Nearest the water were storehouses and animal pens. Most homes clustered around the base of the meadhall's mound. The locals threw rushes in our path to lessen the mud and sang songs celebrating the return of their king's son.

The long wooden hall was magnificent; tall, with a graceful curve to the peak like an upended ship. Appropriate to a sea-faring chieftain. Its elevated position exposed it to the bitter north winds, so there were only two entryways. The servants' access was at one end near the kitchen and slave quarters. The main doors were in a protruding foyer near the centre of the building.

Servants stood at the beautifully carved oaken doors to take our burdens. We stacked our swords, shields and cloaks in the foyer, then received tall cups of ale as we entered the great hall.

A fire crackled in the central hearth, and dozens of oil lamps lit the room. Even so, it took a long drink from my cup before my eyes adjusted to the dimness. If the outside was impressive, the interior was exquisite. Every beam and post carved to depict beasts, flowers, trees or waves in angular, geometric designs. Thick tapestries covered every wall, embroidered to portray stories of Finn's ancestors. Age-smoothed oaken tables with fur-covered benches stretched the length of the hall to either side of the hearth. At the end of the hall, Finn's table stood on a raised platform, draped in brightly coloured cloths, with tall yellow candles in silver holders. Youths played upon pipe and lyre from the shadowed corners.

Our arrival was anticipated, if not the precise day, so platters of fruits, nuts, cheeses and breads were laid out while villagers were recruited to prepare the feast. Our attention focused on the good ale as Hnæf and Frithuwulf became reacquainted with Finn and Hildeburh at the head table. Fifty-eight of Finn's foremost warriors and councillors joined us in the hall. For diplomatic parity, the rest of his retinue went elsewhere. We lounged, getting to know our hosts, trading jokes, stories, and news. Graceful lasses wandered the hall, keeping our cups full and appearing anywhere voices grew too excited, redirecting and cooling our passions.

Ah, it promised to be a grand Yule!

When meat was served, we all took seats, interspersed with Finn's men. Being Hnæf's second captain, I had one of the seats closest to the head table. As I ate, I studied our hosts. Finn was grey-bearded with a kindly face, soft voice and easy laugh. It was clear his people loved him. Hildeburh, Hoc's firstborn, was at least ten winters older than Hnæf, but the fading of her beauty was still far off. She was somewhat aloof, perhaps careful to maintain the dignity of her majesty amongst us coarser men. Hildeburh was every bit the peace-weaver her marriage sought and demanded.

She seemed distant to her brother beside her. Hnæf had said he barely remembered her, as she was married off when he still hugged his mother's skirts. Frithuwulf, beside his father, also seemed uncomfortable. These may be his people, but he had spent his formative years with Hoc's family, and his affections were clearly confused.

Finn's warriors were mostly of Frisian stock, though I caught the accents of Saxons, Franks, Jutes, and even a Geat from far beyond Frisia. No Anglii, though. Perhaps that should have been a warning.

With bellies sated, Finn's scop, a battered old warrior missing an eye, took the floor to recite Finn's lineage. Hildeburh served mead to her lord and those at the upper table, and then she and the other women took their leave.

The mead-jug went round and round as the scop entertained us with bawdy poems, and we joined in raucous songs. Drink and laughter encouraged ever more lewd jests and implausible boasts, inevitably turning to the ancient art of insult. Every man, be he ceorl, captain or king, is fair sport. It is a measure of the man to not only laugh along at his own expense but to serve back better than he received. Finn was a master of the art, laughing at a poem about his age and offering a hilarious rebuttal regarding his warrior's noxious flatulence.

Eventually, it was my turn. One of my younger men, Ealdræd, stood and lifted his cup to me. "Hail, Hengist, son of Wihtgils, son of Witta, son of Wecta, son of Woden! May your sail never slacken!" He took a drink, and I waited, grinning. "Unlike your misshapen misused meagre manhood!"

I joined the laughter and table-banging that rewarded Ealdræd for his alliterative wit. I was about to stand and respond when my eye caught that of a young man across the hall from me. One of Finn's warriors, he rose slowly, leaning forward with his hands on the table. I hesitated, perplexed by the intensity of his glare.

"Wecta, son of Woden?" His voice rose with him. Accent of a Jute. "Kin to Wihtlæg?"

The room quieted.

"Aye." I raised an eyebrow and lowered my chin, guessing the source of his ire.

"Wihtlæg? The butcher of Amloth, king of the Jutes?"

"King of the Jutes?" I feigned confusion, choosing my words carefully. "It's been long since the Anglii permitted a Jute to be called king. Who is this Amloth? And who are you to show such poor manners?"

"I am Garulf, son of Guthulf, Amloth's heir."

"Ah, of course . . . Amloth, the usurper. That war is long past, Garulf, son of Guthulf."

"Murder, theft, and exile make for long memory."

"Mind your tongue, boy," I growled. "Slandering my kin may call for justice."

"Justice? Amloth's father—appointed by your king— was murdered by his own brother, and your king ignored it. Amloth brought justice to the murderer, and the people proclaimed him king–"

"The Anglii subjugated your people long ago. Only our king appoints governors to the Jutes. Amloth flouted that law and paid the price."

"If Wihtlæg knew anything of justice, he would have affirmed Amloth's rule. Instead, he brought war to peaceful people, coveting their wealth and using Amloth as the excuse!"

I leapt to my feet and slammed my cup on the table, splashing mead across the boards. "Boy–" I glanced to the high table. Hnæf was alarmed and spread his fingers out on the table, signalling me to calm. Beside him, Finn looked distressed. Tension was thicker than the smoke in the rafters. My men looked ready to rip Garulf in two. I took a breath. "We are guests of your liege, Garulf. There ought be no quarrel between us over the actions of our forebears. There are many of your tribe amongst my own warband." I held my cup out to be refilled and raised it towards Garulf. "Let you and I drink and be friends, as well."

"Friends?" Garulf picked up his cup but paused at chest height. "Prince of the Anglii to Prince of the Jutes?"

"Aye." It would mean nothing to call him a prince.

"Then you will acknowledge my family's injury? Support restoring me to my legacy and my people?"

I stared at him. Whatever his youth and impulsiveness, Garulf had manoeuvred me into a trap. I could not, here before royal witnesses, advocate his return to his ancestral lands. I could not admit, here before all, that I had no authority to do so. That I had no standing in my own family.

Garulf raised his cup above his head and raised his eyebrows, waiting.

"I cannot."

Garulf's face turned red as he tipped his cup over and let the mead pour out. "You are as wicked as all your perfidious kind!" he shouted and threw his cup at me.

I easily ducked it, but the room erupted. Benches went over, cups and bowls clattered to the floor. Sigeferth, my man nearest Garulf, reached out to seize him but was intercepted by one of Finn's warriors. Finn's man beside me, a Frisian, looked at me, bewildered, then was seized by one of Hnæf's men. Above the brawl, I heard Hnæf and Finn calling for order until a shrill horn blast silenced the room.

Eyes turned to the high table, where everyone stood, looking at Finn. The old king stood on his chair, chest heaving, eyes flaming, a short, white horn in his grasp.

"Cease this mischief! My hall is a place of peace. Order yourselves!" He glowered at Garulf. "You call yourself a prince, Garulf? Even a ceorl knows not to provoke the guest of his master."

"Hnæf is your guest," Garulf retorted, bleeding from his nose and teeth. Sigeferth had landed a good one. "He should know better than to bring dogs into his host's hall."

Shouts again from my side of the hall, while bodies surged on the other. Finn sounded his horn again.

"Enough!" Finn roared, seething. When a tense calm settled, he continued. "Garulf, take your men and go to the docks. You will stay in a storehouse tonight to ponder your place."

When Garulf started to protest, an older warrior pulled on his shoulder and whispered in his ear. Garulf tensed and spun on the man, mouth opening in anger, then blinked. The old warrior whispered to him again. Garulf's eyes flashed back at me, then down to the floor. He turned to Finn and gave a short bow.

"Apologies, my Lord. This was not the time for such words." He spun on his heel and stalked out of the hall, followed by the old fellow and several others.

Finn sighed, stepped down from his chair and threw the horn on the table. He looked around the room, his brow furrowed, then turned and put his hand on Hnæf's shoulder.

"My apologies, kinsman. I am deeply embarrassed. My folk have better manners, and I try to impart them to the foreign warriors who serve me, but sometimes youth requires more than example to learn by."

"Bitter words will be forgotten when heads have cooled," Hnæf replied. "I am certain we will laugh together at the absurdity when next we all gather." He glanced at me, and I nodded in return. There would be no trouble on my account.

"True enough, though heads will cool more quickly if we adjourn and find quiet beds apart." Finn called out to his men: "I will go to my wife this night. Leofstan, take the men to the lower hall. Hnæf and his shall take their rest here in my own home." He turned to Frithuwulf and held out his hand.

"Erm . . . Father, might I stay here tonight?" he pleaded. "One last time with my friends and uncle."

"Of course, my son." Finn smiled. "I was fostered, as well. It is hard to say goodbye."

As Finn and his entourage gathered their things and left, a servant at the back of the room scurried out, returning with a troop of slaves. While the slaves cleared away the rubbish and brought in blankets and woven mats for our beds, I signalled Hnæf and approached the servant who stood at the back door, supervising. The old fellow eyed me warily and nodded a greeting.

"A bit livelier than most evenings, eh?" I smiled at him.

"'Tis true, Lord. How may I be of service?"

"That man, Garulf. Is he prone to provoking guests?"

"Eh, he's known to be spirited, but I've not seen such a display before."

"I saw he has men of his own. Are they all Jutes? Can you tell me how many?"

His lips pursed, and he shifted uncomfortably. "Eh, well, Lord, I, erm . . ."

"I'm not asking to know all your king's strength." I pulled a silver earring from my belt pouch and held it between us. "I only want to know what kind of threat Garulf might pose before we depart."

The man glanced over my shoulder, licked his lips and snatched the earring from my fingers. "Some two score,

Lord. All folk of his homeland." He slipped his prize into his shirt, nodded and stepped away to pretend he was busy directing the slaves.

I returned to Hnæf, who had watched me from the corner of his eye while chatting with the others. After a moment, Ordlaf distracted the group with a funny story. Hnæf tilted his head towards me and whispered, "What did you learn?"

"Garulf has about forty men, all Jutes. He's spirited but not known to pick fights."

Hnæf nodded. "He's not likely to pick another fight with us, then. At least, not on his own."

"It may depend on his standing among the Frisian warriors."

"And that we don't know." Hnæf pondered the doors, tugging on his moustache. "In any event, I doubt Finn will invite young Garulf to mix with us again."

"Forgive me, Lord. I would have stayed on my ship had I known my presence would cause trouble."

"Nonsense." He clapped me on the shoulder, laughing. "This is why I wanted you, Hengist. Things are never dull with you around."

I grinned and went back to the men, reassuring mine and thanking Hnæf's. All assured me that they would never have let the upstart touch me. Many asked questions about his complaint. I could tell them little more than they heard in our argument. It was long ago, but I assume his family went into exile after Amloth's death and maintains the grudge to this day.

Everyone found a place on the floor for their bedding, and most settled in while a few stayed up, sitting in pairs or threes, chatting quietly. I pulled the blanket over my head and tried to sleep, but it would not come. Finally, when the hall had gone silent, I got up and went out the back door to the barrels to relieve myself. Returning, I saw that Hnæf and Frithuwulf were not in their beds. I went out the main door to find them sitting on a bench against the hall, watching the moon skate through silver-edged inky clouds. They nodded a greeting as I joined them, pulling my cloak around my chin to ward off the biting wind.

"Is anyone sleeping tonight?" Hnæf asked.

"You can't hear the snoring through the wall?" I said, prompting chuckles from both.

"It may be my duty, but I would rather return with you in the spring," Frithuwulf said, continuing a conversation I had interrupted. "I don't know anyone here. Even my parents are strangers."

"It won't take long for you to feel at home here and make new friends," Hnæf replied. "Everyone wants to be the prince's friend. Especially the girls." He winked.

"I'd sooner be a warrior in your retinue than a prince in this windswept wilderness."

"Here you'll have your own retinue, your own ship, your own chance to sail and find adventure. Just like Hengist, here." He elbowed me with a grin.

I smiled and kept my silence. I had never told Hoc or his son that I was exiled. Only a few of my original crew remain, all sworn to secrecy. I will return home someday after I am greater—no, I have always been greater than he. I will return when I am richer and more powerful than my brother. Then I will lure away all our people and leave him lord of an empty hall, king of a hollow realm.

The moon went behind the clouds, and Frithuwulf leaned forward and looked out to the east.

"How long have we been up?" he said. "Dawn can't be approaching already. Oh! A house is aflame!"

We followed his eyes and saw a glow to the east.

Hnæf leapt to his feet and dashed to the door. "Those are torches, not a house fire. Garulf intends woeful deeds!"

I was on his heels, Frithuwulf behind me. Hnæf burst through the door and shouted, "Awake, my warriors! Battle comes! Don your mail! Grasp your shield! Bear yourselves proudly and strive for valour!"

None questioned their lord, leaping up and scrambling for their arms, armour, and boots.

"Get tables against the doors," I ordered some of the quicker men. "Wait—go out to the kitchen and bring back all the food and drink you can grab!" Hnæf nodded his approval. We might face a siege.

As some brought in casks of ale and haunches of meat through the side door, others dragged tables to position for barricades. Sigeferth called out that the tables were too long to manoeuvre against the doors.

"Then we'll use benches and shoulders," Hnæf said. He turned to Frithuwulf. "Sister-son, you must go." He started tugging the lad towards the door. "You need not fear. Their enmity is for us, not their liege's son."

"No!" Frithuwulf pulled away from his grasp. "Don't send me away. I would stay here and defend my uncle from wrongful attack."

"They're close," Sigeferth called over his shoulder from his post in the doorway.

"I cannot put your life at risk." Hnæf started pulling Frithuwulf to the door again. "I brought you here to your family–"

"You've been my family for more of my life than they have," the boy protested, trying to pull away. He could not break his uncle's grip, but when the doorway glowed from light outside, I yelled for Sigeferth to bar the door.

Sigeferth slammed it shut and leapt back as Eaha and a few of Hnæf's men shoved benches against the door, then braced it with their arms.

Not a moment too soon. A roar from outside preceded a crash that shook the walls and almost pushed the men off the door. More rushed to lend their weight to their fellows' efforts.

"Too late now," I called to Hnæf, sprinting for the servants' entry, through which Ordlaf and Guthlaf ran with sacks of food. They dropped their burdens and threw the door shut. We wedged tables against it just before running footsteps preceded bodies slamming into it.

Amid the shouting outside and the grunts and heaving breaths inside, a rumbling voice carried through the wall. "My Lord, let your warriors be in the front. Your life is too precious to risk at the door!"

"Does he mean Garulf?" Eaha grunted. "Or Finn?"

The pressure on the doors eased, the shouting ceased, and only heaving breathing and the scuffing of feet remained. We listened, straining for any word to suggest what would come next.

Any thought that Finn led this attack was put to rest when we heard Garulf call out, "Who bars the door of my liege's hall?"

"I, Sigeferth, a famed prince of the Secgan, bar this door! Where is your liege? Does he sanction this violation of hospitality?"

"My bloodfeud is not his concern," Garulf responded. "Neither is it yours, unless you keep Hengist from my wrath. Send him out or share his woe!"

Grumbles rose from my men, and Hnæf's Danes looked to their lord, wondering if he would risk their lives for me. I need not have worried. Hnæf slowly shook his head.

Loyal Sigeferth had no doubts. "Many woes have I endured, and bitter battles. Seek your fate here. I will provide it!"

Garulf must have been prepared for such a reply for, moments later, his men hit the door. Ours, listening to the conversation, had relaxed their efforts and the sudden onslaught caught them off-guard. I could not see what was happening in the alcove, but it was apparent that we were fighting desperately to keep the enemy out.

My attention was pulled back to the servants' door as Garulf's men renewed their attack there. Ordlaf and the rest of our group were better prepared, so the door was not breached. Still, spears thrust through the gap, gleaming steel searching out flesh, while their wielders tried to lever open the door. We hacked at the shafts with our swords and shield edges and threw our weight into our brothers' backs to push the door shut.

A change in the tumult—elated shouts from our men and cries of anguish from outside—drew my eyes back to the alcove. It was choked with our men and, for a moment, it seemed they had found a respite from their struggle. Then the noise outside rose, and the enemy redoubled their ferocity. Moments later, we faced the same heightened assault, and the reason was shouted across the hall: Garulf was slain!

We could give little thought to the news as the press of enemies forced the door enough that one of Garulf's Jutes began pushing through the opening, shield first, protecting his head. It was too crowded to slash over my fellows so I went low, between their legs, and searched out the Jute's lower extremities with my sword. He kept his legs away from the door as best he could, but my blade met resistance and we heard a howl of pain. The man's shield drooped, and Guthlaf smashed his shield's edge down on the exposed head, dropping him. Unfortunately, the body wedged the door open, and another foe pushed further in.

A brutal struggle followed for what felt like an hour but surely was not. The enemy's determination was admirable, but we held as the bodies piled up—theirs, not ours. None of ours fell, but everyone near the door was bloodied. I had only a cut across the back of my sword hand. I might claim that Hnæf and I lead the best fighters in the world, but must admit that defending a door is far easier than breaching one.

We had left our spears in my ship, not expecting to need them, so we played a dangerous game in trying to yank the enemy spears out of their hands. We managed to win a few. Often, we fought over the corpses—or pretended to. We wanted the bodies out of the opening so as not to prop open the door. So we'd shout about who wanted what plunder and start dragging at the bodies. That was enough to make the Jutes pull their own dead away for us.

Finally, the attack ended—suddenly, as if called off rather than from exhaustion. We slumped to the ground to catch our breath and bind our wounds. A bucket of ale went round, and we grinned at each other. Boasting would come later. If we found a way out of this hall with our lives. That was the question on all our minds.

Ordlaf and I joined Hnæf and Frithuwulf, sitting on a table near the alcove. Ordlaf reached across to hand me a drinking horn. He winked and said, "We've earned a bit of mead this evening."

"That'll be the earnest payment," Hnæf said, staring at the door. "Garulf's death may well have sealed our fate. There is no bargaining with a dead man."

"Finn is lord here," I said, glancing at the boy. He looked pale but determined. "Garulf's warband may wish to carry on the bloodfeud, but Finn will bargain."

"I don't think Finn is here—or at least was not until this lull." Hnæf squinted at the door. "Finn will be pressured by his oath to his warband and by Garulf's men demanding vengeance for Garulf's death."

Hnæf was right. The foundation of the bond between warrior and warlord was their shared oaths. The warrior swears to obey and protect the warlord. The warlord swears to reward them generously and lead from the front. If the warlord dies, his warriors are honour-bound to avenge him, or die in the attempt. Anything less results in life-long shame. Garulf had obviously kept his side of the oath. It was unlikely that his men would turn away from theirs. Particularly under the eyes of the Frisian warriors in Finn's retinue.

"We've killed some few of them already," Ordlaf said. "If they decide to fire the hall, we'll be driven out and slaughtered."

"Finn would never let them burn down this hall." Hnæf shook his head, chuckling. "No, they either starve us out or force their way in."

"We have food for a week, at least. Twice that if we go lean," I said. "We won't last that long holding the doors as we did tonight, though. They may not burn the hall, but they'll eventually break down the doors."

Hnæf nodded. "Fortify the space around the doors. Let us invite them in just far enough to die, and no further."

We set to work moving tables into the alcove. We had no axes to break them up, and our swords would have been poor instruments against the heavy wood, so we stacked them on their sides, at angles in the small space, to form an interior wall. The benches provided a place to stand to gain height over our attackers. Fortifying the servants' door was more difficult without the support of the foyer walls. We set the tables closer to the door and piled more furniture to brace them.

We had nearly finished when someone banged thrice on the main door and called out in a tired voice: "Hnæf, it is Finn, your brother. Open the door and return me my hall."

"Your men violated hospitality," Hnæf shouted back. "Where were you? Did you sanction this?"

Finn's voice lowered. "You know I did not. It grieves me that an old bloodfeud has shattered the peace."

"The bloodfeud died with Garulf, did it not? Send your thegns away, and we will talk peace."

Silence for several breaths.

"The bloodfeud may be over, but Garulf's men demand his slayer."

It was just as Hnæf had predicted. We looked around at each other. In the confusion of the melee, no one knew when Garulf had been struck down, much less by whom.

"Hnæf? What say you? Name the man who killed Garulf and save the lives of many."

Hnæf stood and looked around the room, face grim. I felt a pang of fear and guilt. None of this would have happened if not for me. He would be in his rights to send me out. His gaze settled on me, and I knew my doom approached. He turned back to the door and shouted, "I, Hnæf, slew Garulf! And I will fight unto death any who seek to take me by force!"

A tumult erupted outside until we heard Finn shouting for silence. The commotion faded, and we listened to quiet for a long pause.

I was stunned. Hnæf had taken the burden of their revenge upon himself rather than sacrifice a single man sworn to him. Tears came to my eyes. I wished I had been born to his family rather than mine.

Finally, close to the door, we heard Finn speak again. Just loud enough for us to hear him. "Frithuwulf. Are you well?"

Frithuwulf looked to Hnæf, who nodded towards the door.

"I am, Father."

"Come out, my son. I vouchsafe that no harm will come to you, and my men will make no attack while you do so."

Frithuwulf licked his lips, his eyes darting between the door and Hnæf.

"You are free to go to your father," Hnæf said. "There is no slight to your honour for doing so."

Frithuwulf shook his head and stood, summoning his most confident voice. "A warrior is sworn to his liege above family, Father. I have not yet left Hnæf's service and taken up yours. I must remain here until you end this wrongful assault and guarantee the safety of every man in this hall."

Another long pause. When Finn responded, I had to strain to hear him.

"Hnæf . . . Safeguard my son."

Hnæf lifted his sword so that Finn could see the hilt. "On my sword, Hildeleoma, no harm shall befall him while I breathe."

If nothing else, that guaranteed they would not burn the hall down upon us.

There was no further sound from outside. We prepared for a renewed onslaught, but none came. After a full log had burned away on the hearth, Hnæf sent one of the men to open the door and peek out. A spear nearly took him in the eye. He slammed the door shut and vaulted back over our makeshift wall. Still nothing happened.

"They hope to lull us into slackening our guard on the doors," Hnæf told the men. "You have fought like heroes.

Keep heart. None of us has more than a scratch, while no few of theirs are dead for their efforts."

We established a watch and dozed in our armour beside our wall, weapons close to hand. When the assault came again, it must have been shortly before dawn. This time they were able to break down the barriers we wedged into the door, and it must have surprised them to find their way barred nearly at the doorway. Unable to push further into the hall, they faced three of our men to every one of theirs. It became an outright slaughter.

And yet they persisted, watering the thirsty earth with their blood. How many, we could not know. It seemed every warrior of Frisia had come to kill us.

*

The fifth morning dawned as all the others, with an attempt to push through our makeshift walls. It did not last long. The last few days had seen the attacks come with less enthusiasm.

I sat on the floor against a post, waiting for the next foray and watching sunlight move across the dark rafters. Both doors were destroyed and a frigid wind whipped through the hall. We had food enough, but little fuel, so we endured the cold and saved the wood for cooking.

The wind was preferable to the stench that settled during calms. We could not leave to attend nature, so emptied casks served us until they overflowed. Sweat, blood, and vomit added to the reek.

Five days of hopeless bloodshed had numbed us. There was little speech. None of the jokes or games men engage in, even in hard times. Just exhaustion and grim determination to fight until cut down.

It was inexplicable that none of us had fallen, though we all bore wounds. Mostly minor, though a few men lay beside the hearth, too injured to raise spear or shield. Frithuwulf was the exception, of course. Hnæf refused to let him near the fighting. The boy accepted it sullenly, chewing his nails on his father's throne—one of the few unbroken or unburnt furnishings left in the hall.

Hnæf sat beside the hearth, poking at a small mound of coals with a broken spear shaft. I had never seen him other than cheerful. The days had turned him as taciturn as the rest of us.

Eaha brought me a hearth-cake and a few pieces of cheese, pressing them into my hand when I shook my head. I opened my mouth to curse him, stopping when I saw the concern in his eyes.

"Eat," he said. "Enfeebled men don't lead men."

I grunted and flicked a piece of cheese into my mouth. He sat beside me and leaned against the post, handing me a battered copper beaker of ale. I wondered how this clash would be remembered. Whether the scops would tell of it. Whether my people would hear of it. I dozed.

The call of the watchers roused me. Finn's thegns coming on yet again. We staggered to our feet and went to the walls. I went to the foyer, where the fighting was always thickest, and called hollow words of encouragement to our men.

We traded blows with the enemy, fending off their spears and responding with our few captured spears. They had learned to avoid coming within reach of our swords. Ordlaf, beside me, ducked just in time to avoid taking a savage thrust in the face, but it caught on the helm's ridge and punctured the steel. I caught him as he stumbled off the platform, blood sheeting down his face.

I pulled the helmet off and dropped it. Its clatter caught Hnæf's attention.

"How bad?" he called, batting away a spear with his sword.

"Hold still," I muttered, trying to examine the wound on the tall warrior's forehead. He struggled to wipe the blood from his eyes. Hnæf appeared over my shoulder. "Just the skin," I said. Head wounds tend to be bloody and painful. Ordlaf sputtered and gritted his teeth.

"Set hot iron to it and get back to the wall." Hnæf turned to go back to the fight.

"How can I fight with such wounds?" Ordlaf moaned. "My mail is rent, barely hanging on my shoulders. I'm near blinded!"

Hnæf turned back, his eyes showing the battle within himself. The leader won out over the friend, and he pointed back to the wall. "How do those warriors endure their wounds?" He pointed to the two who had taken our places on the wall. "Which of those two young men can take your place as champion to inspire the others?" He shook his head when Ordlaf opened his mouth. "Answer that for yourself." Hnæf ran back to the battle, leaping high with a shout to bring his sword down upon the head of a man climbing the wall. Our men cheered, and Hnæf's example renewed their vigour.

I held out my hand. Ordlaf grimaced, nodded, and we went to the hearth. Several old knives were already heated to glowing red for just such a need. Ordlaf lay down and put a piece of leather between his teeth. Two others came to hold his arms. I sat on his legs and, before he could think more about it, pressed the blade to the wound.

The flesh sizzled and seared, and Ordlaf bucked like a feral bull. The leather shot from his mouth, propelled by a bellow of pain that echoed through the hall.

No, it was not just his howl. I turned back to the battle at the foyer to see our men in a panicked cluster where Hnæf had stood. They struggled over something against more foes than had yet managed to push into the space.

Hnæf!

Our king was limp, half over the wall, being pulled in opposite directions by our men and theirs. I cried out and leapt up, leaving my sword behind in my haste to keep them from taking Hnæf.

A shape blurred past, nearly knocking me aside. Frithuwulf launched himself at the enemy, hacking with his sword, tears streaming down his face as he shouted curses.

Just as I got my hands on Hnæf's leg, a spear reached out and took Frithuwulf in the throat. The boy stumbled back, off the platform, landing on his backside. He looked down, confused by the blood pouring over his chest. His eyes turned glassy, and he slumped to his side.

The scene around me took on a sort of other-worldliness, as if time slowed and sped in random moments, the noise of battle muted. I felt my knees weaken, then my grasp. When Hnæf's ankle slipped through my fingers, I awoke. I seized his foot, screaming in rage, pulling with all I had until we yanked him from the enemy's grasp and fell to the ground.

I reached for Hnæf's face, but Ordlaf appeared, shoving us away from his lord. He knelt beside him, cradling Hnæf's lifeless head, rocking, tears flowing.

The battle was over. All eyes were on Hnæf and Ordlaf. The only sound was the wind through the hall and the panting of our men. Just beyond the doorway, the dark profile of a man's head showed above the wall, looking in at us.

"Have you dogs had your fill of vengeance?" I shouted at him, then pointed at Frithuwulf's body. "Tell your king his son is dead!"

The form disappeared, and we were left alone to stare at the corpse of all our purpose. Our lord was slain, and we still lived. Custom would have us charge out to avenge Hnæf's death or fall in the attempt. Scops sang of ideals. Legends. We faced reality, and reality had exhausted us.

We laid Hnæf and Frithuwulf on the king's dais and cleansed them as best we could. Then we sat and stared at them. If Finn's men had attacked, we would not have been prepared. Instead, we heard the patter of slippered feet and the screech of a woman restrained.

We stood, and several went to the wall. They could see nothing but reported the sound of hushed, urgent speech outside. After a short time, a lone set of footsteps crackled on the frozen ground before the door.

"It is I, Finn, son of Folcwalda. Dreadful tidings have come to my ears: that my son, Frithuwulf, and my wife's brother, Hnæf, have fallen. Tell me this is untrue."

Ordlaf and I looked at each other. Without Hnæf, Ordlaf must speak for the Danes. I could speak only for my own men, and this was a family issue.

"Someone speak!" Finn shouted, his voice cracking. "Is this true?"

I raised my eyebrows to Ordlaf and tipped my head towards the door. He took a breath and called out, "It is true. They are both dead."

A woman, surely Hildeburh, screamed. It sounded as though she were struggling and beating on a shield before her cries fell to sobbing. After a time, we heard footsteps approach again.

"I wish to parley," Finn said. "Who within has the authority to treat with me?"

Ordlaf and I went to the wall, but I waited on the floor as he stepped up to look out.

"I, Ordlaf, son of Hunlaf, will hear you." He motioned for the others to step back and stood there alone. I watched through a crack in the wood as Finn shuffled into the foyer, unarmoured and leaning on a staff. Perhaps it was the wan winter light, but the king looked more aged and bowed than when we first saw him five days before.

"How did my son die?" Finn croaked.

"A hero," Ordlaf replied. "Hnæf would not let him near the fight, but when Hnæf fell, Frithuwulf leapt to avenge him and fell to a spear."

Finn's head bowed, and he stood there for a long spell, swaying slightly. When he finally spoke, it was little more than a whisper.

"I did not want this. I could not convince Garulf that there was no honour in this feud. Nor restrain the others from supporting him out of loyalty."

Finn went silent again. Ordlaf fidgeted and looked at me, uncertain. I gestured as if sheathing a sword. He nodded and turned to Finn.

"Will you accept terms to end this bloodshed, O King?"

Finn raised his head, eyes red and swollen. "What terms might restore my son to me?"

Ordlaf's expression turned hard. "We did not slay your son. We did not bring this bloodshed. All we may restore to you is your hall and your peace. If you want neither, you can be assured that we will fight until the last man stands, and he shall burn this hall down as our pyre."

Finn looked down, nodded. "Peace must be enough. What are your terms?"

Ordlaf took a breath and gazed at the men around him, then through the opening to the bright sunlight. Finally, he said, "By this chill wind and the frost on the ground, it is clear that the winter ice will be upon the sea. We must rely on your . . . hospitality . . . until we may sail home in the spring." Finn nodded, and Ordlaf continued: "Swear to keep us under your protection and provide us ample good food and drink. Give us a separate hall for my folk and Hengist's to share, close to Hengist's ship and easily defended in case your people cannot be restrained." He motioned for me to join him on the platform. "Swear this to both of us."

"I will do all this and more." Finn straightened and raised his voice so that those outside would hear. "I will honour you as my own thegns, with gifts of silver, gold, and jeweled treasures. And this my councillors proposed: that by my oath, any who bring violence against you also bring it upon me. I decree that no man shall by word or deed impugn you for following the slayer of your patron, as necessity, not disloyalty, has laid this fate upon you. If any of my people violate my decree, the edge of the sword will make good the pact."

Ordlaf looked at me, relief in his eyes. I felt misgivings, but when I looked back at my men, I saw guarded hope in their expressions. I nodded.

Ordlaf seemed to shed a weight and turned to Finn. "Swear oaths to this pact, and we will come out."

Finn turned and went to the door. He leaned his staff against the wall, and someone handed him his sword. He unsheathed it and held it aloft as he made his oaths for all to hear and, when finished, sheathed the sword, slamming it home with finality.

There were no cheers. No songs. Just the wind whistling through the hall. Finn said a few quiet words to someone, handing off his sword, then came back inside. He stood there, looking at us as we stared back, until Ordlaf started, then nudged my arm and stepped down from the wall. I followed and motioned for a few men to help dismantle our barrier. We soon cleared enough away to create an opening for Finn to pass through and prove he would keep his word.

Finn walked slowly through the hall to the dais where Hnæf and Frithuwulf lay before the thrones. He sank down between them, laid his hand on his son's chest and sat there, head bowed, white hair hanging down around his face.

We watched silently for a long time until some of the men became restless, and their movements distracted Finn. He sighed, stood and walked back to the door. "Gather your belongings. A place is prepared for you." He then disappeared outside.

We had little to gather. Many stuffed food into their pouches, still not trusting Finn to keep his oath. I confess I pocketed some cold meat while looking at the bright portal to a world I thought I would not see again. Oaths be damned, we all expected to walk out to a slaughter.

When all was ready, we laid Hnæf on a board, and several men hoisted him to their shoulders. We would not leave him behind. Ordlaf and I led the way and were the first to exit. We stopped a moment, eyes dazzled by the mid-morning sun. No steel bit us.

When our eyes adjusted, we found Finn and his men in a silent cluster well to our left, shields and spears at their feet. Relief was overtaken by shock. The frozen ground was stained red for a hundred paces from the door. A closer look at Finn's warriors showed nearly all to be old men and young boys. Hildeburh was nowhere to be seen.

Where were the mighty warriors of his household? Were they in hiding, waiting to ambush us? I glanced at Ordlaf, whose eyes showed the same fears.

Finn gestured, and one of the young soldiers shuffled toward us. Pale, wide-eyed, his voice shook. "Lords, I will show the way to your hall."

Perhaps the boy knew he was the sacrificial calf in Finn's plan. I looked at my fellows, then myself. Perhaps it was our monstrous appearance: filthy, grim, and covered in gore.

We followed him down to the village. Several plumes of smoke rose near the western beach.

"What is that?" I asked the boy.

"Pyres."

The burg seemed empty. No men carried burdens through the streets. No women beat out the bedding. No children dashed from house to house. Every door was shut tight. Only the dogs eyed us from a safe distance, growling. I loosened my sword in its sheath and shared a wary glance with those near me.

The boy turned towards the docks on the east side, and as the end of our column entered the village, a woman's wail rose from Finn's hall. Hildeburh must have found her son.

We reached the edge of the village and walked along the shore. Most of the boats were beached, but mine still bobbed beside the dock near the warehouses. I wanted to examine her, but splitting up would make us even easier prey.

When the boy stopped beside one of the larger buildings, we drew our swords and clustered together, ready for the attack. The boy fell on his face in terror, raising his hands in supplication.

I pulled him up by his tunic. "Are they waiting inside?"

"Who, Lord?" the boy stammered.

"Finn's thegns!" I shook him. "Where are they?"

"On the p-pyres, Lord." His thin arm pointed to the smoke rising in the west.

Ordlaf leaned down and looked the boy in the eyes. "All of Finn's hearth troops are dead, you say?"

"N-nearly all, Lord."

Ordlaf and I looked at each other, dumbfounded. Those boys and old men were Finn's army, bereft of his best warriors. The narrow confines, dim lighting and necessity for our men to rotate through guarding our doors had concealed the extent of their casualties. Garulf's men and the Frisians had thrown themselves against us like rage-blinded boars.

Ordlaf's eyes narrowed, and he pushed the boy toward the door. "You'll go first. If there is any trickery, you'll die first."

The boy shook like a leaf but opened the double doors wide and entered. There was enough light to show what appeared to be an empty storehouse converted into a hall. Tables and benches lined the sides, and a simple, low hearth was laid out with stones in the centre. An old woman sat there, coaxing a fire to life.

We stared, confused. This was not possible. Yet, there it was. The old woman stood, head bowed. The boy gestured for us to come in, looking relieved and eager, as if he had been unsure what to expect when opening the doors.

We stumbled inside, suddenly feeble when released from the exertion, tension, and dread of five days of bitter battle. We laid Hnæf at the far end of the hall, where his seat would have been, and crossed his hands over Hildeleoma's hilt upon his chest.

There were double doors in each of the other three walls, and the place had the stale, dusty smell of an old threshing barn. The boy and the old woman laid out food and drink while we found places for our belongings; Ordlaf and his folk on the right side, me and mine on the left. As we ate, they warmed water for us to bathe, and the boy gave us blankets so the woman could take our clothes to wash. She also gave us clean linen bandages to bind our wounds.

Clean, fed, and wrapped in a blanket by the hearth, I started to nod off. I forced myself to my feet and shuffled around the fire to nudge Ordlaf, who had fallen asleep. He groaned and sat up.

"That boy looked surprised to see this place empty," I said.

Ordlaf grunted. "I suppose we should set a watch."

I nodded. "Do you believe his best men are all dead?"

"Hard to believe. But, either way, he could only starve us out or burn his hall down around us. He didn't want to lose that hall, and once we ran out of food, our only option would have been to cut our way out. If that lot is truly all he has left, we may have made it."

"Maybe we should take the fight to them first."

"Tonight?" Ordlaf looked around the hall. "With the state of our men, old men and boys are just as good as hearth troops."

I looked around the hall. The rest were sleeping, or on the verge. It would be a hard thing to even keep anyone awake for a watch. "Not tonight. But we can't defend all four doors in this dry old barn. I doubt he'd fret over losing it to rid himself of us."

"He can't burn this place." Ordlaf shook his head. "The other buildings are too close. The whole village would go up."

"You think we're safe?"

Ordlaf shrugged. "I think the Fates will have us when they will."

I sighed. "You want the first watch or the second?"

II

A Broken Rope

I thought I would sleep soundly that night, but my peace was disturbed by all manner of strange visions and fretful omens. I woke to a bright ray of sunlight piercing the gap in a door where the man on watch sat just outside. More apprehensive than I had been the night before, I bundled myself in my blanket, eased the door open and stepped out. The man on guard there was one of mine, Ceolmund.

He nodded a greeting and yawned.

"Anything to report?" I asked, squatting down beside him.

"Quiet all night, I was told. I caught a glimpse of a boat rowing out there a bit ago." He pointed to the southeast. "Coming this way, but went more to the west."

"Not likely to be fishermen," I said, looking at the beached boats.

Ceolmund shook his head. "At least in Finn's hall, we knew what to expect from these Frisians."

I stood, clapping him on the shoulder. "More importantly, they know what to expect from us." Always appear confident. He grinned in response, and I went back inside.

Not much later, the old woman returned with several other matrons, carrying food, drink, and our clothing, cleaned and folded. The boy came soon after with a message that Finn was sending fine wood for a pyre for Hnæf, and that he and Hildeburh would attend if we did not object.

If we did not object.

Ordlaf, Guthlaf, Eaha and I were sitting together, discussing what to expect from Finn when the boy made the announcement. We sent him outside and stared at each other. A night of rest had rekindled Ordlaf's fury. Guthlaf saw the look on his brother's face, looked at Eaha and me, then nudged Eaha and stood.

"Eaha and I will go outside with the boy to find a suitable place for Hnæf's pyre," Guthlaf said.

"We'll tell the boy we do not object," Ordlaf growled. "Then I kill Finn and throw him at Hnæf's feet."

I wanted to tell him what we both knew. Such a violation of the funerary rites would lay a curse upon us so black that others would shun us for fear of being caught up in the Fates' vengeance. But I could not form the words. Not with Hnæf lying there beside us. A lord so brave and generous that he would have conquered the world by drawing all its warriors to his service. Had he not been cut down at the dawning of his manhood.

"We do not object," I agreed.

I stood and helped Ordlaf to his feet so we could find the boy and give him the message. At the door, Eaha nearly collided with us.

"Two ships coming this way," he whispered. "Guthlaf wants to know what to tell the boy."

Ordlaf looked at the ground. I said, "We do not object to Finn and Hildeburh coming, with the expectation that they will bring trophies appropriate to honour Hnæf."

Eaha nodded and went back out. Ordlaf still stared at the ground, jaw clenched.

"We bide our time," I said. "Finn will race against the weather to bolstered his ranks to a strength we cannot overwhelm. It does us no good to insult the king."

Ordlaf spat then nodded. "Fate will be revealed in its own time."

I released a tense breath, and we went out to the chill morning. I shielded my eyes from the morning glare and saw the two ships disappearing behind the land to the north.

"If they're coming here, Finn must have them beaching near his hall," Ordlaf said.

I nodded, looking out at my ship resting at the dock. I was inclined to bring it out of the water and inspect it, but we might need to get away, sea-ice be damned.

Guthlaf and Eaha came up from our right and hailed us.

"The clearing over there." Guthlaf pointed to a space on the shore to the south. "Should do well for Hnæf's pyre. Might need to move a couple boats."

"Show us," I said. "Then we'll walk around a bit to learn our surroundings."

"I poked around a bit this morning," Eaha said. "I'll wait here to show them where to stack the wood."

Ordlaf was right about the buildings being too close to risk a fire. Those nearby were storehouses and workshops, though no one was working this day. On our walk, we saw some villagers, never less than a stone's throw away, and each hurried away when they saw us.

We returned to our "hall" and spent the remainder of the day discussing ways to fortify it quickly when—if—needed. I sent my men to gather our spears and spare shields from the ship while Ordlaf's men prepared Hnæf's pyre.

As sunset approached, Finn's messenger returned with word that Finn and Hildeburh would arrive shortly, and that a feast was being prepared that would be brought to us after.

The men gathered what few trophies we had snatched during the battle while Ordlaf and Guthlaf prepared Hnæf for the funeral.

Dressed in our clean clothes, our panoplies patched and polished as best we could, we raised Hnæf on the plank and marched out to the beach. The area was cleared and the pyre stood near the high-water line, though the tide was out. Our men formed a double line, the Danes on the right, my men on the left. Ordlaf, Guthlaf, Eaha, and I carried Hnæf through the line. The men reached out to touch Hnæf, offering quiet words of farewell, until we reached the pyre and placed Hnæf upon it. As we arranged our trophies around him, Finn and Hildeburh appeared, leading a host of Frisians onto the beach.

My stomach knotted. Finn must have called up the fyrd to have so many armed men so quickly. Even the presence of Hildeburh and other women in the procession did nothing to allay my fears that the Frisians would attack now that we were out in the open.

They may have come to cheer on our murders.

Our men crowded together, apprehensively watching the oncoming throng.

"Faces of stone, my boys," I called out. Ordlaf and I needed to show leadership before any chance of chaos. "And straighten those ranks. We are hearth troops! Not a rabble of farmers called up for the fyrd!"

The men straightened the ranks and stood proud. If blood must spill, Frisian blood would fill the bay.

Finn held up his hand and they all stopped well beyond a spear's throw away. He motioned and walked forward with Hildeburh. Four warriors stepped out of the group bearing a plank with a body. Frithuwulf. They followed Finn, and a dozen slaves, backs bent under their burdens, came from behind Finn's soldiers and followed them to stand before us.

Finn looked tired and greyer. Hildeburh was wan, with red eyes sunken in dark hollows, yet her face was as blank as one of those statues the Romans scatter about. Finn gestured to the slaves.

"I have brought trophies to adorn Hnæf's pyre," he said. "May this be the first token of peace between us, men of war." The slaves laid down piles of rent and bloodied mail, riven shields, cloven helms, broken spears, cups and bowls of gold and platters of silver.

We gaped. So much lay before us, there was no doubt Hnæf would stand proud before the gods.

Then Hildeburh lifted her head and stared directly at Ordlaf. "Lay also Frithuwulf, my son, beside my brother, so that they may rise on the flames together. May this be the first token of reconciliation between us, family and thegns." Her poise showed why she was a peace-weaver.

Ordlaf acquiesced by bowing his head. Finn's men placed Frithuwulf beside Hnæf and laid out his gifts while our men arranged the funerary offerings around Hnæf. Many a wary eye shifted between the groups, and they avoided standing too closely.

When all was done, and the red sun was low in the western sky, one of Finn's men lit a torch and handed it to the king. Ordlaf tensed and would have stepped forward to object if Finn had not immediately turned to him and offered him the torch. Ordlaf accepted, and I wondered if Finn could sense the grudge in Ordlaf's bearing.

We all lit torches from Ordlaf's and took our places around the pyre. Ordlaf raised his torch, then thrust it into the twigs and sticks bundled under the heavier pieces of wood on which Hnæf and Frithuwulf lay. The rest of us did likewise, then stepped back. The flames raced through the fuel and engulfed the pyre, the smoke heavy with the sickly-sweet stench of burning flesh.

Hildeburh burst into tears, wailing a mother's lament. The other women joined her, their song mourning the loss of all they labour to create. The men stare, silent, to contemplate our own inevitable climb upon the smoke. Such is the custom of all who speak our tongue, whether Frisian, Geat, Angle or Jute.

When their song faded to wails and moans, some of the Frisians began to trickle away. We watched beyond sunset, until the flames consumed the bodies and the pyre collapsed in on itself, signalling the departure of our lord's and Frithuwulf's souls. Finn clasped Hildeburh to him and turned away, followed by the rest of his people, leaving us alone on the beach. Eaha took on the uncomfortable burden of being first to turn away so that Hnæf's kin could show their familial loyalty one last time. The rest of my men followed, myself last.

I entered our hall to find my men drooling in anticipation of a great feast laid out for us. They waited for me, and I would wait for Ordlaf and his folk. We may now be masterless, but these Danes had bled beside us. We will not forget.

When Ordlaf and Guthlaf finally returned, last of all, the men were nearly mad with hunger. We set to eating and drinking, grim at first and mostly silent, until the fine food and drink turned the night merry. We had lost our lord—we saluted the fallen—but we had not retreated or abandoned him. We had stood our ground, forced a capitulation from our attackers. Our defence of the hall would be sung for generations.

Ordlaf's mood lightened, but he still brooded. I, too, felt uneasy. Perhaps all this fine food and drink was for nothing more than to lull us into lowering our guard.

Ordlaf must have read my thoughts. He stood and called out, "Listen, you all! We are not at home here. Do not gorge yourselves, nor take so much drink that you can't stand the line if need be." He tossed the contents of his cup into the fire. The sizzle and flash of the mead on the coals underscored his words.

He stepped around the hearth and sat heavily on the bench beside me with a grunt.

"You hate seeing others happy, don't you?" I smirked.

"Just you. I'm going to spread the rumour that it was your idea."

I chuckled, then gazed at the fire a moment. "Finn seems sincere. That was not local wood he sent for Hnæf's pyre."

"He flaunts his wealth."

As if in response, the door opened, and the boy who led us here entered and announced that the king was coming. The room turned tense, the men looking to us to see what they should do.

Before anyone even had a chance to go for their weapons, Finn strode through the door. Behind followed a pair of his older warriors, perhaps councillors, and several slaves carrying large bundles.

"My good men," Finn said with a careworn smile. "As promised, I come to honour you with gifts such as I give my own thegns." He motioned, and the slaves cut the cords on their packages. "I pray you do not find them wanting."

I found myself on my feet. Firelight shone on silver, bronze, and gold. Twinkled on gems, glowed on furs, ivory, and amber. His false humility was the loudest boast I had ever heard.

"You do us honour, king." I bowed, nudging Ordlaf to do the same. He stood slowly, surprise showing on his face, and bowed as well.

Finn nodded, gesturing magnanimously, and stepped over to one of the piles. He lifted a golden cup with gems and pearls decorating the swirls and lines that covered its surface. "Ordlaf, son of Hunlaf, I give you this ancient cup of my kinfolk." He held it out. "May it bring you health and good fortune."

Ordlaf hesitated, then walked across the room to take the cup, bowing. "I will remember you when I drink from it."

Finn's eyebrows twitched, but he smiled as Ordlaf returned to his seat. He next picked up a fine woollen cloak, white as snow. It had large gold shoulder clasps, ornately carved and decorated with garnet.

I hungered for that cloak. Would it go to Guthlaf, or . . .

Finn turned towards me and held it out. "Hengist, son of Wihtgils. A cloak fitting for a man whose lord held him in such high esteem."

I may have appeared less dignified than Ordlaf as I strode to receive my gift. It was magnificent. "I will wear it proudly, Lord."

I scarcely noticed the gifts the others received as I admired the cloak's workmanship, bright garnets and clever fastening pins. Ordlaf managed not to glower as Finn doled out his treasure and, when finished, the old king wished us a peaceful evening and departed. The tramp of feet outside the hall indicated that Finn had not come without protection.

"That was a brave show of trust for Finn to leave his guard outside our hall," I said to Ordlaf.

"Or arrogance."

"You still doubt him? Even after these kingly gifts?"

"Trinkets. No mail. No blades." Ordlaf's eyes went to the door. "He need only murder us to regain them."

"Well, if he wants these back, he won't be able to burn the building down on us."

Ordlaf grunted, half-smiled, and ambled off to mix with his men. I stared at the door, thinking of my ship.

*

Winter is good for thinking. The long, icy nights inspire brooding. I tried not to fret about our circumstances. Sailors often dream of homecomings when stranded in foreign lands, but that refuge was denied me. I steered my thoughts instead to reminisce on my travels. The length and breadth of the East Sea, all the coast of Germania, much of Gaul, and up the many rivers to the interior.

I found myself pondering my progeny, a subject I rarely gave thought to. I've certainly sired some few offspring in my travels, though I only know of one for certain. A daughter named Rothwen. Her mother, a northern Jute, has a beauty that has called me back more than once. I last saw them some two years before, when the girl was about nine. Golden-haired Rothwen favours her mother. Were she born of higher stock, she would undoubtedly grow to be a peace-weaver like Hildeburh.

Even these pleasant thoughts did little for my mood. I slept poorly unless I drowned my senses in ale or mead, which Finn provided amply. He visited regularly, at least on each Woden's Day, handing out gifts as generously as he had after Hnæf's funeral. I marvelled at Finn's courage. Or wondered if he could be so blind to the tension.

Ordlaf's fury cooled. Not like boiling water, but like a heated blade: sharp, even if no longer glowing. On the surface, he was as calm as an inland sea. Knowing him was like feeling currents rage against the hull beneath your feet.

I felt no fury. I struggled to feel anything but foreboding. Perhaps Ordlaf's mood washed over me. I struggled to put forth a sanguine air, as a leader should. I put the men to work because idleness breeds trouble. Daily exercises and swimming in holes cut into the ice. We explored Finn's lands and villages, going in pairs or threes so as not to raise alarm.

Before the ice overtook the harbour, we pulled my ship from the water and made repairs as the weather allowed. Finn provided wood, pitch, rope; all I asked for.

When not working or honing their martial prowess with wrestling, boxing, or weapons practise, the men ate well of fine food, played at games of chance or strategy, carved walrus ivory, or enjoyed the women that Finn sent to brighten our hall. The Yule passed as well as any man could ask. Despite the lingering gloom.

The men were uneasy. The whispers that came to my ears echoed my own thoughts:

We live in the hall of the slayer of our lord. Is that not a dishonour?

Finn was innocent in the conflict and generous in making amends for the sins of his servants.

Could he not restrain his own thegns? Prevent his Frisians from aiding the Jutes?

Perhaps the bonds between the Frisian thegns and Jutish exiles were no less strong than those between the Danes and us.

We are oathbound to slay Hnæf's slayer. A lord is responsible for his men's actions.

Finn has too many warriors here now. And we made a pact of peace with Finn.

The ancient law of hospitality was violated when we were attacked.

Is the guest no less bound to the law than the host?

There could be no reconciliation between the two arguments. Nor the turmoil within my heart. Ordlaf and Guthlaf whispered to me of honour, vengeance and loyalty. Tied to Hnæf by blood as well as oaths, the Danes were inclined to vengeance. My men swore oaths to me; were bound to Hnæf only for love of me. Those few who would speak their mind to me did so. Most wished to enjoy the bounty of Finn's wealth and then go in search of a new patron in the spring.

The spring. Every winter has that time when it seems the thaw will never come, yet it always does. I was eager to float my ship and sail away with my men. Salt spray on my face and new lands before my eyes might salve the ache for my dead friend.

As that time approached, I set the men to readying their kit, mending the sail and inspecting the ropes with the help of Ordlaf's folk. One night, as they slept, I sat on a bench beside the hearth, staring into the fire. Ordlaf appeared beside me and stood there a moment, staring at the fire before turning to face me.

I looked up at his face. It was no less haunted. No less conflicted. But his eyes held a purpose that I longed to feel. Holding my gaze, he leaned down and placed something across my knees. He stared at me as if to penetrate my soul, then squeezed my shoulder and walked off to his bed.

I looked down and saw the sword across my knees, golden hilt and ivory grip glowing in the firelight. Hildeleoma. Hoc had given it to Hnæf just before he died. It is the finest sword I have ever seen; its deadly edge famous among the Jutes who tried to oppose the Danes' settlements on the peninsula.

I broke. Tears long damned by frustration and indecision poured forth. I shook silently, head bowed, my dusky hair hanging to hide my face.

Ordlaf had said more with that sword than with any of his words. I owed Hnæf my loyalty. Even more so, his father. I imagined Hnæf standing before Hoc in Woden's halls, both ashamed that the son had not been kingly enough to inspire the loyalty his father had. This, I could not abide. Hnæf had died childless. If the Hocing line was ended, it deserved a glorious passing.

I pondered long that night. Men stirred with the morn, and I had not slept. But I had gained a purpose and a plan to see it through. I woke Ordlaf, and we went out, exiting the village through the drover's gate to stroll the fallow fields and pastures to the south. By noon we were back at our hall. Then I slept as I had not slept since we arrived on this cursed island.

*

Two nights later, Finn came for his weekly supper visit. When the musicians paused, and Finn was about to distribute the customary gifts, Ordlaf stood and asked to speak. Finn nodded graciously, and Ordlaf bowed.

"Lord, familial relations brought us hither with good will. Misfortune wrought tragedy, and while we made peace, we've been obliged to remain under your generous hospitality through the winter. Spring has come, the sea is clear, and it is time for Hnæf's remains to return to his home."

Finn nodded and said, "I knew the time was near, though I regret to see such valiant warriors depart. You may be assured that I will lade Hengist's ship with treasures and offer sacrifices for your safe voyage."

"You are gracious, Lord, and generous . . ." Ordlaf paused and glanced at me, vexation showing on his face.

I stood and addressed the king. "My Lord, my service to the Hocings is over. I wish them well, but my men and I must lay a new course." I fidgeted. "However . . . until I've plotted that course, may we remain here?"

A smile of relief creased Finn's face. "Yes. Yes! You are my guests and may remain as long as you like. Ordlaf, I will provide a ship and crew to speed your folk home."

And the die was cast.

*

The following week passed in a flurry of preparations: a ship and crew, provisions, the packing of gifts and personal belongings. The night before the Danes set sail, Finn attended the feast and gave out more lavish gifts, including a large silver urn for Hnæf's and Frithuwulf's ashes. We stayed up late into the night after Finn retired; my men and the Danes recalling our shared experiences, proclaiming our fraternity and wishing each other good fortune.

The next morning, Finn and Hildeburh came to see the Danes off. Finn splattered horse blood on their prow and offered the requisite prayers. Hildeburh draped a garland of flowers over the stern, and paused to lay her hands upon the great silver urn that held her brother's and son's ashes.

"Frithuwulf and Hnæf exemplified loyalty, affection, and honour," she said. "It is fitting that they share their final rest together. Let it be an example to us all."

Rumbles of concurrence answered her. We said goodbye to our brothers-in-arms and watched the Danes join Finn's sailors aboard the vessel. They shoved off, and the ship moved out to the channel with a rhythmic slap of oars on the water. Ordlaf waved once from the stern and I answered, then turned and walked back to our hall, feeling emptier than ever I had known.

*

Without the Danes, our days were dulled. I kept up our normal routines, including our walks around the island. I ensured my men offered no insult to anyone or their property. The townsfolk had become accustomed to us and did not shrink from our approach, but often gave a greeting or offered their services in barter.

Finn came to our hall on his accustomed day, with gifts to give, musicians to play, and women to dance. Laughter flowed as freely as the mead, and I suggested Finn bring in some of his men to join us. Finn was delighted. A dozen of his leading warriors shared songs and drink with us, and when Finn was ready to retire, we all parted as if there had never been war between us.

"That was a risky gambit," Eaha murmured as the Frisians filed out of the hall. "Of course, if any of the attackers still lived, Finn was wise enough not to invite them into the hall."

"Fences are mended one post at a time, my friend." I smiled, but from the corner of my eye I could see the dubious look he gave me. Eaha is one of the few who may speak his mind to me at any time. I was glad he decided to forego the privilege that night.

*

When Finn returned the following week, I offered twenty-seven seats for his folk to share our table equally with us. Finn bade me sit on his right, and we talked through the night.

At first, it was the usual talk, of trade, farming, fishing, and family. It turned, inevitably, to the topics that men of war most ponder.

"These are dark times, Hengist." Finn drained his cup and motioned for a slave to refill both of our cups. "Far too dangerous for kith and kin to clash."

"I did not know that a prince of the Jutes was amongst your warband, Lord." Yet I should have known. The Frisians and Saxons, as well as the Jutes, were all too happy to see the Anglii pressured by the Danes moving into the Juteland. For those Jutes unwilling to submit to Hoc and his people, the Frisians were their natural allies.

"Had I known of your heritage, I would not have brought Garulf to the feast. I am stricken to have found a feud within my own hall."

"You could not have known, Lord," I said soothingly. *That was true enough.*

"It might still have gone otherwise had I not so shamed Garulf by sending him to the fish-house." Finn hung his head and shook it. "He saw no other way to preserve his honour. I should have known. Now, my son and nearly all my greatest thegns lie dead."

And Hnæf.

Finn took my silence for sympathy and patted my arm. "Had I such warriors as you and yours, my people would have nothing to fear."

I did not expect his courtship quite so soon, but there it was. He would not invite me to his service tonight, but he was cutting the path. So, I teased the hook. "You are the most powerful king in Frisia, Lord. You must have little to fear."

"Oh, fear always weighs heavy on the ruler. Always. If not a pestilence or plague, then drought or war. Even now, some terror from the east drives every nation westward in desperation. The pressure of it lies upon our borders."

"What is this terror?" I had heard rumours but played the part of the naïve youngster to the grandfatherly king.

Finn shrugged. "A horde from beyond Scythia. Strange people who never walk the earth, living out their lives on horseback. Warriors who drink blood and make their clothes from human skin."

"And if they come this far?"

"We have some protection on our islands, but the seas are rising, drowning much of our farmland." His eyes drifted to some distant memory; his hand stroked his beard. "I have given thought to new settlements for my people in Britannia."

"The Roman island?"

"Rome abandoned Britannia a score of years past. The inhabitants are few and timid. We often raid their lands, and each year my warriors must row further up the rivers to find plunder." Finn drained his cup and thumped it on the table. "But my head grows heavy, so such thoughts must wait for another day."

*

The second and third weeks passed much as the first. Mutterings arose amongst my men, questioning our future. Warmer than usual winds invited us to raise sail, but all marked Finn's solicitousness. They suspected I would take service with the king. Some were for the idea, some against. All watched me and waited.

In the fourth week after the Danes departed, Eaha found me on the beach and sat down.

"The men grow restless," he said.

"I know."

He was silent for a long spell, then said, "A lesser captain would have lost men by now. Too long without direction and the most energetic will leave in search of purpose."

I nodded. We continued to sit in silence. I could feel Eaha's agitation simmering. "A purpose will reveal itself," I finally said. "My mind rests on little else. If I were to mention one prospect or another, it would unleash endless questions, fruitless speculation, or premature chatter that might spoil any plans or negotiations."

"I knew some scheme was forming." Eaha grinned. "I'll counsel patience."

"Quietly. The best course is to act as if there were none." Eaha nodded, and I lowered my voice, staring out to sea. "You know the abandoned homestead to the north?"

Eaha glanced at me, then looked away. "About an hour's walk from here?"

I nodded. "One of us, perhaps a few of our more discreet comrades, should pass it daily. If they see a broken rope tied to one of the old dock pilings in the cove, they should continue on their way as normal, then report to me at supper, mentioning it to no one else."

"I've not walked that way in a few days." Eaha stood and stretched. "I think I'll check on the ship and go for a stroll."

I watched Eaha walk away. I called him "Warhorse" because he was steady in any situation. The name stuck, and now no one called him by his birth name. A man could ask for no better friend.

*

Four days later, Ealdræd came to me at the evening meal. I glanced at Eaha, who watched us from the corner of his eye. Ealdræd did not come to me first.

"Lord, I walked north along the shore today," Ealdræd said. "I saw a frayed rope tied around a piling."

"Hmm . . ." I handed him a piece of bread. "How many times did the rope loop around the piling?"

Ealdræd blinked, and his mouth fell open.

"Think, man. How many times?"

"Erm . . . just once."

"You're certain?"

"Yes, absolutely. One time around and knotted."

"Very good, thank you. Keep this to yourself."

The following day, I went out with the men to float the ship, check the ropes, look for leaks, test-fit the mast, raise and lower the sails; all the tasks needed to prepare a vessel. I was shaving a block of wood for a wedge when Finn showed up. His advisors and guards stayed on the beach as he walked out on the dock to join me.

"You've charted a course?" he asked.

"Not entirely." I set down my work and stood. "A dream told me to see where the winds take me."

"Last night?"

I nodded, and Finn raised his hand and looked about. "The winds are still today. Perhaps the meaning is for you to remain here."

"Pledge my sword to you?"

"Have I not been generous? Have I not shown you and yours honour? Have I not demonstrated every quality of a worthy lord?"

"You have, Lord."

He noted the hesitation in my voice and put a hand on my shoulder. "You need fear no dishonour for taking service with me. I have dismissed the sad remnants of Garulf's band. You would be honoured here as one of my chief thegns." He grinned. "And if you think I am generous to my guests, you must see how gold rings spill from my hands for those who serve me."

I smiled and nodded, then looked wistfully out to sea. "May I give it thought for a day? I should speak to my men, to see if any are against this."

"Of course. A good leader does no less." He paused. "Perhaps, after your deliberations, you might all come to my hall tomorrow evening and share my table, as we have visited yours?"

"If they're not opposed, and I don't think they will be, that would be a fine thing."

"Excellent!" Finn beamed. "Then I will await your response."

After Finn and his men departed, I motioned for Eaha to join me. He picked his way across the deck, grinning.

"Eaha, go for a walk today. Take along a wineskin and when you get to the abandoned farm, sit by the fence and have some food and the wine. Leave the emptied skin hanging on the fence and return."

"It will be done," he said. "Will there be an explanation of all this someday?"

"Sooner than you expect."

Eaha nodded, grinning, and walked away to the hall.

I looked to the evening meal with apprehension. It would likely turn contentious. I had made my decision. How many would remain with me?

*

The next night I led my men—all of them—to Finn's hall. Not all agreed with my decision, but not one would leave my service. My heart overflowed with love for these men.

The setting sun glowed red on Finn's hall as we climbed the hill. We walked to the door between a double line of Finn's soldiers. Twenty-eight, to match our numbers. Ostensibly to show us honour, but mere prudence in reality. Such was proven by a tent erected outside the door that sheltered a stack of shields and weapons. Our shields and weapons joined those, and the porter led us into the hall.

Finn sat at the head of his table, Hildeburh beside him. Twenty-eight of his foremost thegns and councillors stood at the tables below, an empty seat beside each so that we might join them as brothers. My seat was at the place of honour, first below the king, beside a wizened old warrior who now served as Finn's foremost councillor. Finn's men acted as if there were never a moment of discontent between us. Finn welcomed me as warmly as if I had grown up around his table. Hildeburh remained aloof.

The heaping food and free-flowing drink turned the evening so boisterous that Finn's musicians gave up on their pipes and lyres. When the servants cleared the food away, they also took the table in front of Finn and his queen. It was time for Finn to bestow gifts.

It was a lengthy affair, as Finn started with the lowest ranking of my men, then his, and alternated through all, coming closer to his dais, and to me. The old man beside me nudged me and grinned,

"If you think these gifts are lavish, you should see what he heaps upon his thegns!"

I grinned and nodded, and tapped my cup to his.

Finally, all had received their gifts but me. A slave handed Finn a small bundle, and the king waved me forward.

"Hengist, son of Wihtgils," he said, unfolding the cloth on his lap. "This is an ancient treasure." He held up a bright gold neck-ring, the ends shaped like fish-heads, with scales carved along the body. "A fitting token for a man of the sea."

I accepted the gift and bowed. Finn did not wave me back to my seat. Instead, he leaned forward and spoke in a quiet voice.

"Have you considered my proposal and taken counsel?"

"I have, Lord."

"And your decision?"

"Would you fetter us here? Or send us out upon the seas to bring you fame and riches?"

"If such is your desire, you may join my roving fleets, fill your holds with plunder and bring your king glory."

I knelt before him and bowed my head. "I could pledge my sword to such a king."

I could feel the glow of Finn's smile as he called to his porter to send my sword. I felt a bit lightheaded. I listened to the sounds about me. The crackling of the hearth, the shifting of men in their seats, belches, slurp of drinks, clink of cups, the footsteps of the boy bringing my sword, Finn shifting in his seat to take the sword and turn back to me.

"Receive this sword, Hengist son of Wihtgils," Finn said, drawing my head and eyes up to see Hildeleoma extended towards me. "And let us speak the oaths of fealty and patronage."

I reached out and laid my hand upon the scabbard beside Finn's hand. Hildeburh, who had been gazing indifferently across the hall, glanced towards us and gasped.

"That is my brother's sword," she said.

Finn glanced at her, then the sword, then me, his expression shifting from surprise to puzzlement to horror. I grabbed his wrist and wrenched the king from his dais, spinning him. My left hand grabbed a fistful of his long white hair, and my right snatched Hildeleoma from the loosened scabbard he clenched.

Hildeburh screamed. The room erupted in shouts, knocked-over tables, struggling men, the sound of knives in meat, death screams. The pair of guards who stood in the shadows behind Finn's throne leapt forward but stopped when they saw the steel I held to their king's throat. The sound of struggle behind me ceased, replaced with heavy breathing, gurgling coughs and moans. The coppery scent of blood overwhelmed the hearth smoke. Someone banged on the hall's door, shouting for the doors to open. Finn's slaves were rushing out the kitchen door.

"Throw down your weapons!" I barked at the two soldiers. They stood a moment, uncertain, until Finn dropped the sheath and showed them his palms. They laid down their swords and watched anxiously. Several of my men rushed to take the weapons and shoved the guards towards the kitchen door.

"Stop this!" Hildeburh cried, standing. "Are you mad?"

"Stay in your seat, Queen," I said. "I do not wish to hurt you." She stood where she was, fists clenched at her sides, pale but seething.

As my men shoved the guards outside and barred the kitchen door, Finn spoke in a calm, quiet voice.

"I have treated you and your men as if you were my own. Now, you treacherously spill blood in my hall? What do you seek? Vengeance? If you kill me, you must know there is no escape."

"Escape is not my aim," I said, turning the two of us to face the tables. Finn choked back a cry. I pushed him down to his knees and kept the sword at his throat.

The floor was awash in blood. Twenty-eight Frisians lay dead, sprawled on the floor or across the tables. Some of my men secured the main door while the rest stood over their victims, grasping the knives they had kept concealed.

The banging on the door intensified, with more voices raising the din. Eaha directed the men to barricade the doors with tables and add their weight.

"What is your aim?" Hildeburh sobbed. "Have you not wrought evil enough here?"

"I did not bring whatever evil lurks in this hall!" I shouted at her. "It dwelt here before ever I set foot upon this land!"

"Have pity," Finn said. "She has lost son and brother, kith and kin, all too recently."

The pounding on the door became the heaving of shoulders trying to force it open. The shouting outside increased, a sure sign that all the warriors in the village were rushing to their lord's aid. Some of my men looked to me, trying not to show their apprehension, but the tension stood out in their eyes and lips.

Finn and Hildeburh continued to talk. He, in measured, quiet tones. Hildeburh strident, pleading. I comprehended nothing they said. I wanted them to be silent, but I could not speak. I could not sense the passage of time. My eyes roved to the doors, to my hand holding the sword at Finn's throat, to the loyal men I had surely doomed.

I began to wonder if we might walk out with the king and queen as hostages. Then the muffled sound of distant horns came through the walls. The shouting outside withered to silence. The door no longer shook. Finn and Hildeburh fell silent.

A new commotion began, of distant cries and ringing bells. Hope renewed. My men erupted in cheers. Some moved to tear down the barriers, but I called for them to stop.

We waited, anxious, and straining to make sense of the sounds outside. They waxed and waned, but ever louder, closer. After an eternity, the noise of battle was clear, rushing suddenly upon the hall's very threshold. The struggle beyond the doors was bitter, but the clash of steel and cries of the stricken quickly fell away to silence.

Finally, we heard a pair of hard raps on the door, and a voice called out: "Hengist! Are you asleep from gorging on mead and bread? Let your comrades in!"

I laughed, the tension falling away, and responded, "Boredom put us to sleep, Ordlaf! Waiting so long for your army to arrive."

My men unbarred the doors and swung them wide. A red glow lit the foyer, and through it strode Ordlaf, Guthlaf and another man, followed by a dozen more, armed and covered in the gore of battle. The movement of many more could be seen outside. I let go of Finn and embraced the new arrivals.

"This is Hrothgar, Hnæf's kinsman," Ordlaf introduced me to a young lad. "His men raised havoc in the village while Guthlaf and I set the trap for Finn's soldiers."

"It was simple," Hrothgar shrugged, "with the southern gate unlocked and all of Finn's men pounding on the door to his hall."

"The time we took to explore the lands and villages made it easy to disguise the army's approach," Guthlaf said.

"And now the hall is yours," I said, handing Hildeleoma to Ordlaf.

He took the hilt and stared at it as if seeing it for the first time.

"Ordlaf . . ." Hildeburh's voice shook.

Ordlaf took a step forward and plunged the sword into Finn's chest. Hildeburh screamed and rushed from her chair, only to be intercepted by Guthlaf and Hrothgar. Finn's mouth opened; he spasmed and fell onto his face as Ordlaf yanked the sword out.

"Justice is done," Ordlaf said, looking down at Finn's body, fresh blood flowing out over old.

"Justice?" Hildeburh cried. "This is no justice! This—"

"Vengeance, then." Ordlaf glared at her. "Fulfilling oath and honour. You might give that thought." He turned to me and offered the sword's hilt.

"No," I said. "It should remain among Hnæf's people."

"You won't return with us?" Ordlaf looked surprised.

"I'll come to see Hnæf laid to rest, but then . . . I think it's time I find a home for myself and my men. Become a lord in my own right."

"I see a different fate upon you," Hildeburh shrieked. "Any home you claim will ever be soaked in treachery and blood. Your line will end. No people will claim you as forebear." She spat at my feet.

I felt the blood drain from my face but acted as if I had not heard her.

"Bah!" Ordlaf scowled at her. "When did you become a seeress? I see no staff in your hands. Save your wind to fill our sails and speed you back to your people." He motioned, and Guthlaf and Hrothgar guided the protesting woman out of the hall as gently as they could.

Ordlaf turned back to me and grinned like a child at Yule. "Now let us gather the spoils. You'll be rich enough to found an entire dynasty."

*

We pillaged Finnsburg until the sun rose. Ordlaf and his folk filled my boat with more treasure than I could have imagined, and still there was plenty for the hundreds of warriors they brought on a dozen ships. There was so little room to spare that even slaves were dispensed with.

Before the Frisians could muster their own army, we sacrificed the prisoners and rowed for the sea. Finnsburg smouldered behind us; the survivors long fled.

With the wind in my face and the rising sun at my back, I lost myself in wonder at barrels filled with gold and silver cups, platters, and bowls. Stacks of furs, woven rugs, bronze vessels, iron bars, swords, helms, mail, shields. I ran my fingers through a chest of amber, glass beads, and varied gems; another of gold rings, brooches, and delicate chains.

Ordlaf was right. I could raise my own army with so much wealth.

We reached open sea, and Sigeferth steered us to the north as Eaha prepared the ship to ride the wind. Ah, there are few things so glorious to see than a fleet raising sails on a red dawn!

Eaha returned from inspecting the rigging and leaned on the railing beside me.

"It's good to feel the waves underfoot again," he said.

"Did you think we might not survive to sail again?"

"No." He smiled, looking down. "I sense Fate is not done with you."

"Yet, you're uneasy," I said. "Don't deny it. We know each other too well."

Eaha frowned and fidgeted, and finally looked me in the eye. "I fear what curse we might have brought down by killing our host."

"We did not kill our host." I shrugged. "But more importantly, what curse might we have earned for not observing our oath to Hnæf?"

Eaha grinned and nodded, slapped the railing and went to see that the oars were properly stowed.

What remained unspoken was Hildeburh's curse. I doubted she held such power, and I refused to lend it strength by acknowledging it.

*

Our fleet sailed easy, beaching at night to enjoy the food and drink we had taken from Finnsburg. A rainy, week-long voyage brought us to Hnæf's ancestral home on an island in the East Sea, east of the Juteland.

Our arrival was greeted with an outpouring of joy. The villagers prepared a great feast and lavished attention on us. There was no king or queen to lead the celebration, and I did not ask. That was for Ordlaf, Hrothgar, and the elders to deal with once Hnæf had been laid to rest.

We stayed for several weeks. I did not see Hildeburh until Hnæf's remains were placed in the burial mound. She stood apart during the ceremony and spoke to no one, eyes always downcast or staring at the grave. I steered well clear of her.

With the duties of the living to the dead fulfilled, it was time for me to move on. Where to go had plagued my thoughts ceaselessly. My childhood home constantly came to mind. I had left swearing never to return until my brother was dead. Perhaps it was the adulation of Hnæf's people and the riches in my hold that made me think I would be welcome there now. Perhaps my brother was dead. It would only require two or three days sailing to discover the answer.

I rewarded my men generously and spent more to ensure we all were clothed and equipped like princes. The better to impress my estranged kin. We bid farewell to our Danish brothers and their people, then raised sail and turned south.

III

A Reunion

We rowed slowly up the long estuary through the heart of the Angeln, past farms and small villages where people eyed us warily but without dread. That no one appeared to recognize me as we passed did not surprise me. Yet it was disconcerting that these lands looked just as I remembered them. I suppose I expected things to have changed as much as I had after all these years.

The estuary widened into a long bay. In the distance, I could just make out my ancestral hall on a rise above the water's north bank, with the village clustered about. We beached and set camp. Strange warships seldom bring good tidings, so better to let the locals come to you.

I could not make out any activity around the village, but inhabitants from along the river had kept an eye on us. Before long, an enterprising fellow let curiosity and need overcome his fear. A fisherman, he rowed his small boat to just beyond spear range and called out to know if we meant peace and would trade.

I assured him we did and we would. He left a happy man with more wealth than his meagre catch warranted. As expected, others soon rushed to bring us all manner of goods and services. I was generous and encouraged the people to stay and celebrate. Before nightfall, our camp had tripled in size, with ample food and drink, laughter and music. Their goodwill was my buffer against what might come from my brother.

He still lived and ruled. I did not give my name, but asked questions to learn if I was remembered. It was dispiriting to find no one did until, late in the day, some folk from my village started to trickle in. Most were younger than me, but I recognized one old fellow as the carpenter my father had hired to help me build my ship.

"Sæwine!" I walked towards him, arms open. "It's good to see you."

"Hengist? Is it you?" He stopped, mouth open. "Oh, my boy, why did you come back?"

"Even you don't have a welcome in your heart for me?" I was taken aback. I know I had been a headstrong youngster, but I thought old Sæwine had liked me. Perhaps it was yet more of my brother's poison.

Sæwine gave me a nervous embrace. "Of course I do. It's your brother who won't be pleased."

"He has no more reason to fear me contesting his rule now than when he sent me away." I gestured to my men. "Just as I need not fear him."

"You don't understand." Sæwine held up his hands. "Your name has been whispered about recently, and your brother is in a foul mood."

"As I said, he has nothing to fear from me." I smiled. Word of my fame and riches had already reached my brother's ear.

I made sure to entertain lavishly that night. To these impoverished people, it seemed they dined at Woden's own table. We especially targeted the younger men, potential recruits, with gifts and flattery, and told stories about our adventures. Our five-day defence of the hall and subsequent sack of Finnsburg was particularly popular. We celebrated late into the night with great bonfires. My brother could not ignore the spectacle we created on his shores. I fully expected his invitation to appear in the royal hall the next day.

No messenger came the next day. No boats came from my village, though more people from other communities and farms came. It was obvious my brother thought to demean me by ignoring my presence. So, I encouraged even greater revelries that night.

The next day, the sun rose on a camp that might have looked like a battlefield slaughter if the bodies lying about had been dead and blood-covered instead of snoring and vomit-covered. Such was when my brother decided to make his appearance.

I staggered out to relieve myself in the river and saw a dark blotch on the water near the village. I rubbed the sleep out of my eyes, and the blotch turned into three large ships rowing towards the camp. I groaned a curse and went about waking the nearest of my men to get the others up and pre-sentable and clear the locals away from the beach. Then I returned to my tent to wash and dress.

Things were presentable by the time the ships were close enough to hail. My men arrayed behind me, and the locals thronged further back on the slope above the beach. I raised a spear high in the air and, in response, someone on the lead ship sounded the peace-hail upon a horn. Everyone relaxed, if only a bit. If those ships meant war, we would be heavily outnumbered. I doubted my brother would react violently to my return. I was not certain.

The ships rowed straight towards us without slowing until the oars were pulled in nearly simultaneously, and they coasted onto the beach with a scouring rumble. For a long breath, nothing happened. No sound but the water lapping on the hulls and seabirds crying on the wind. Finally, there was a shuffle of movement on the middle ship. My brother appeared at the prow, looking down on me, frowning. The long sandy hair I remembered had retreated to a stringy fringe around his ears, and he had grown wide across the middle.

"I discounted the rumours of your return at first," he said. "The reported debauchery of the last two nights convinced me. It seems your judgement has not improved with age."

"I thought it best to wait for you to come to me, Brother," I said, with my most disarming smile. "If you feared a mere boy, I wouldn't wish to terrify you as a man."

"Fear had nothing to do with why you were sent away." He scowled, crossing his arms. "You were incorrigible; a deceitful little agitator who nearly wrecked several alliances by deflowering any girl who came within reach."

My men snickered behind me, knowing there was likely some truth to that last remark. So, despite the anger welling up in me, I kept my tone light and asked, "Oh, and how is your wife?"

Laughter erupted behind me, and I caught a few snorts from those within his ships. My brother's face turned red and he leaned forward, pointing at me.

"Don't trifle with me!" he sputtered. "You've not changed at all, except perhaps for the worse. News of your treacherous deeds precedes you, Brother."

Silence fell. I stared, suddenly cold. "What are you talking about?"

"Are there so many such deeds? When you sleep, do you not hear the cries of the people of Finnsburg? Those who sheltered you through the frozen months just to be slaughtered when the spring came?"

"We were attacked in Finn's hall, and our liege was slain!" I shouted. "If you knew anything of loyalty, you would know we were oath-bound to seek vengeance."

"Your thin excuse to murder your host and steal his wealth is beneath a noble of this household. You are not welcome here."

"I have no wish to stay. I came to find warriors to join me, to seek wealth and glory in a distant land. Some men of courage must still live in the Angeln." A rumble of agreement rose from the crowd beyond my men. The reaction on my brother's face was worth the expense of the past two nights. "Two ships, and crew to man them. Hard gold will cross your soft palms, and I will never set foot here again."

My brother hesitated, licked his lips. He gazed out at his people, saw that their sympathies were with me. His pride might have stiffened his neck if not overpowered by his lust for gold.

"I will not condone such transactions," he said. "But neither will I interfere. No one who would enter your service is fit for this realm. You have three days." He looked out to the crowd and raised his voice. "Any man who leaves with Hengist is an exile, forever banished on pain of death." He looked down at me with a smirk and turned away. My brother was not the type to let antipathy get in the way of profit.

Shouted orders from the ships were followed by sailors dropping over the sides to lighten the boats and push them back out to deeper water. They clambered back aboard, the oars came out, and the three ships rowed slowly away. I turned to my men but addressed the people beyond them.

"The gods have favoured me with much." I held out my arms towards my men. "But most of all, in the men who sail with me, conquer with me. Whom I proudly call brothers. If you would seek adventure, wealth and fame, join us." I dropped my arms. "Or remain here with your ploughs and nets."

*

Two nights later, I sat on the beach, hoping my brother's sleep was disturbed by the heat of my hatred as I stared towards his hall. I had expected to have my ships and crew within a day or two. Instead, we would sail in the morning with only one additional ship and barely enough recruits to man it.

Plenty of boats were offered, but most were in ill repair or not suited to the work of a coastal raider. More disappointing was the lack of qualified recruits. My brother's poison discouraged many from enquiring. Of those who did, most were the desperate sort, unfit for duty, and even fewer had any experience in battle.

Eaha walked out of the shadows and squatted next to me, handing me a wineskin. "All's ready to break camp in the morning. Where will we find more crew and another ship? The Danes?"

I took a drink. "I was thinking we visit your folk next." I handed the skin back. "You can see your boy while I find another ship. Oeric is old enough to walk the warrior's path, no?"

"He is. Last time I saw him, he was just learning to walk." He took a drink. "Not much farther to where your daughter lives. She must be . . . eleven winters now?"

I took the skin back. "Sounds about right."

We were quiet a spell. Then Eaha said, "Fate is strange. Our path was turned sharply by a fight instigated by Jutes. Yet here you sit beside one. Your daughter is half. Most of your warriors are Jutes."

"And yet more will be." I handed him the skin. "There are many Jutes in the world, my friend. Holding any of you responsible for Garulf's deeds would be as stupid as Garulf blaming me for those of my ancestors."

Eaha took a drink, returned the skin, stood and thumped me on the shoulder before walking away. I was surprised that my closest friend, a brother in all but blood, needed such reassurance. I should have gone straight to his people rather than come here. He must have thought the same.

It was a waste of time and resources to come here. I know not what I expected to find. Certainly not a home. Perhaps only vanity. Show my brother I had become greater than he. No one will remember his name. I will not speak it. Only my name will be remembered.

The swish of oars on the water interrupted my thoughts. A small boat appeared from the gloom and scraped to a stop on the bank a stone's throw away. I caught my name in a muttered conversation, and then a shadow slipped into the water and pushed the boat back into the river.

My hand went to my knife, and I rose slowly to a crouch. Options raced through my mind. If assassination was my brother's scheme, how should I best expose him? Not with a dead man he could disavow. I must take this one alive.

The figure strode towards our camp. I followed stealthily, puzzled by the stranger's brazenness. When he reached our tents, he went directly towards a clearing where a low fire illuminated several of my men lounging and chatting. He stopped and studied the group from the shadows. I prepared to tackle him.

The man stepped into the light and said, "Can someone take me to Hengist?" A youngster's voice.

The startled group rose with questions of: "Who are you?"

Before anyone could say more, I stepped up behind the stranger and laid my long knife at the side of his throat. He stiffened, his hands going out where they could be seen.

"You've found him," I said. "How may I be of service?"

"I wish to join you," he said. "Brother."

"The right to call me 'brother' is earned." I pushed him towards the fire.

He stumbled, then turned slowly around. "Even for your own blood?"

I gaped. He looked very much like me, or at least as I was ten years ago. The same dark hair I inherited from my mother. The long, straight nose I shared with my father.

"You don't remember me." He looked disappointed.

"Horsa?" I scarcely remembered the boy, who was only five when I was exiled. We were both named for my father's passion for horses—one he developed late in life after receiving a pair as gifts from a Roman envoy.

"Yes!" Horsa beamed. "Our brother tried to hide your presence from me. Sent me on a hunt to the south. One of our dog handlers broke his leg, so we returned early. Sæwine told me you were here, and I begged him to bring me."

"You want to come with me? Be an exile?"

"I'll take exile over prison. Our brother fears anyone overshadowing him. I want to see the world, make a name for myself. Be like our father."

I smiled and pulled him into a welcoming embrace. There was no hint of duplicity in Horsa. I would not lower my guard, but it brightened my spirits to have a happy reunion with some remnant of my family.

*

We sailed early the next morning, before our brother could note Horsa's absence and try to interfere.

The voyage around to Eaha's village on the northwestern coast of the Juteland was uneventful. He was excited to see his son, though I could see he was hurt that the boy shied from him, having no memory of his father.

I left Eaha and Sigeferth to manage the preparations and took Horsa with me to visit my daughter, a half-day to the southeast. I gave Rothwen and her mother rich gifts, and we recruited a score of stout warriors, then returned to Eaha's village.

Eaha and Sigeferth had done well, obtaining a third ship and crew. We stayed a few weeks, training the men, collecting supplies, and refitting the boats. I deflected questions about our next destination, saying that I was still forming a plan, which was partially true. It troubled me that Eaha was the only one who never asked about the future. Finally, one evening, as all preparations were nearly complete, I asked Eaha to walk with me. We strolled along the beach, watching the sun approach the grey line of the sea.

"You've done well organising our next adventure," I said.

Eaha smiled and dipped his head in appreciation. "Have you planned the next voyage?"

"We go south, along the coast. Raiding as opportunity presents, but I want to visit the Roman ports in Gaul and have all our men properly equipped."

"An expensive plan. Will you have anything left from the Finnsburg plunder?"

"Little, I'm sure. Yet our future raids will be overwhelming, particularly in Britannia." I nodded out to sea.

"That Roman island?"

"The Roman army is gone, and the people who remain are timid and weak. Yet they still have enough wealth to make rich men of those bold enough to seek it."

My friend nodded, staring thoughtfully at the sand as we walked. I stopped and, after a couple of steps, he noticed and looked back at me. His eyes gave away an inner turmoil.

"What's on your mind, Octha?" He started at my unusual use of his given name, then looked down at the ground. He fidgeted, digging his toe at a piece of buried driftwood.

"I'm torn, Hengist." He looked up and took a deep breath. "The life of a wandering warrior is hard. I . . ."

"You wish to make a home. Raise your son." I had suspected this might be the source of his disquiet. The joy he showed around Oeric was abundant.

"Part of me does. The other wishes to sail the seas with you."

I nodded. "You're my right hand, you know. I'll be diminished by your absence, but I understand you." Was it so different from my longing for family, and my joy at finding Horsa? Did Eaha feel displaced by Horsa's addition to our circle? "With you as his teacher, I'd be eager to have Oeric join our crew when he's of age."

Eaha's eyes brightened. "That's some six years off."

"Surely. But you must come with him."

"Ha! Of course!" Eaha leapt to grab me in a fierce embrace. It eased my melancholy.

Eaha is proof that family is more than blood. It is also an anchor.

*

When we sailed a few days later, we had a full complement aboard all three vessels. Sigeferth commanded the second ship, and Horsa the third. It would do him well to learn by doing, as well as watching.

Such was our confidence that we passed few settlements along the coast without a foray for plunder. We even captured a few trading vessels upon the sea. The Roman towns were larger and more prosperous than those of the Frisians or the Franks. And also better defended. We lost a few men along the way.

For some reason, those losses struck me harder than they would have in the past, despite all being green recruits. I replaced them easily enough. Yet I could not shake the feeling that I was destined for more than wandering piracy.

Late in the summer, we arrived at the Roman trading port of Bononia. The Gaulish coast there comes so near the isle of the Britons that we could see both shores from the sea.

I contemplated options as I browsed the market. We had explored a few sites along Britannia's coast further north, but the only settlements we found were long abandoned. Much of the dwindling treasure I had won from Finn's hoard must have come from those places.

As Finn had said, the opportunities for plunder were to be found further inland. Navigating strange rivers through unfriendly territory was hazardous. Without a guide, we could be whittled away, no matter how unwarlike the inhabitants.

Eaha came to mind again, kindling my thoughts of making a home. If there was so much empty land in Britannia, it should be simple enough to start our own settlement. Eventually found my own kingdom. The land there was more fertile than even our homelands.

I grimaced and spat. The very thought of becoming a farmer! I am a warrior. A reaper of men, not grain.

The hand of Fate guided my rudder yet again. I passed a stall selling fresh oysters. The proprietor, a thin, weathered fellow much older than I, was haggling with a potential customer in my language. I could tell it was not his native tongue, but I stopped when he said his oysters came from Britannia and were exported as far as Rome.

I loitered until their business concluded, then approached the merchant.

"You're from Britannia?" I asked, smiling.

"I am. The best oysters come from Rutubi, near my home. I gathered these this morning. How many would you like?"

I held up my hand and nodded to his excessive price. He grinned broadly, collected five, expertly split the shells with a small knife and handed them to me. I chatted with him about his business, the fishing, and other mundane things while I ate. The oysters were good. I purchased five more.

"I am Hengist." I offered my hand. "You speak my language well. Where did you learn it?"

"Ceretic," he said, taking my hand with a smile. "I was a trader, like my father. I grew up sailing with him, shipping goods from Hispania to the Juteland."

"You gave up trading?"

"Not willingly." He grimaced. "The markets collapsed years ago when Rome stopped patrolling the trade routes. I was just getting by when I lost my ship to pirates. I was lucky to escape with my life and freedom."

"Would you return to trading if you had a ship?" This Ceretic could be the guide we need.

"I'd like to, but without safe sea lanes, it's too risky." Ceretic pursed his lips and thought a moment. "Time will tell. We have a new government, and the Overlord promises to stop the Picts and, well, Saxons, begging your pardon," he tipped his head, "from raiding our lands. He might rebuild the navy."

"No offence. I'm no Saxon." I grinned. "So this Overlord is rebuilding the defences?" This could be a problem.

"Trying to. The problem is manpower. There are too few trained soldiers to man the coastal forts, much less patrol the seas."

Clarity struck me like a rogue wave. Perhaps we could settle a new home and remain warriors.

"Ceretic, we may be able to help each other."

*

My three ships are beached on a small isle the Britons call Tanet. The rain has stopped, and I can see the mainland of Britannia across a narrow channel to the west. Somewhere beyond the mist is an old Roman fort they call Rutubi. Sounds of alarm when we arrived suggested they thought us to be raiders. We sounded the peace-hail, then sacrificed a calf and hung its head on my tent to prove our peaceful intentions.

Ceretic's information had revealed an alternative to wandering that preserves our warrior ethos. The Britons need soldiers. I will offer our service to the Britons' Overlord in exchange for our keep, for patronage and, in time, for lands of our own.

Ceretic, now my interpreter and emissary, lives on Tanet. So, while we encamped, he went off to fetch the leaders of the local governing council. In a short time, he was back, breathless. The councillors were all at Rutubi. Strangely enough, the Britons' Overlord had just arrived there to inspect the defences. Not long after, the Overlord's emissaries arrived and invited me to an audience with the king. Vortigern, they call him.

If I ever doubted the hand of Fate, I no longer do.

The witch was wrong. The Fates don't toy with me. They drive me like their own stallion toward some great destiny.

Hengist's adventures have only begun. See more as the struggle between the Anglo-Saxons and the Britons leads to the rise and fall of the man behind the legend: Arthur, King of the Britons, in the exciting historical fiction series: The Arthurian Age, *published by Perseid Press.*

Acknowledgments

I have many people to thank for being able to indulge my story-teller persona. From the folks who provide me a job to pays the bills that writing doesn't, to the friends who offer support even if they don't read the books, to the kind people on the Internet chat groups who help me research, I wish I could adequately thank them all.

Above all, I must always thank my beloved wife, Jennifer, for her patience, support, and input. I could not do this without you, babe.

I want to thank Ms. Ruth Ann Heusinkveld. She was my high school librarian, and she set the book in my hands that inspired my first published novel, three decades later. She passed away a few months ago. I wish I could have told her sooner. She is proof that librarians make a difference.

I owe a great debt to archaeologist Keith Fitzpatrick-Matthews, North Hertfordshire Museum Curator and Heritage Access Officer. Historical fiction can be a bit of a jigsaw puzzle to assemble, and some of the more obscure parts fitting together are due to his input and kind willingness to answer my many questions. His expertise has had a major impact on the authenticity of my writing.

Thanks to Cas Peace, Jeff Boice, Betty & Duncan Perry, and Andrew Douglas for your beta-reading and editing. You all help make me a better writer.

Thanks to Dmitry Yakhovsky for his fantastic artwork.

And finally, thanks to Chris and Janet Morris. Your mentoring and support have opened a whole new world to me. Your friendship is one of my great blessings.

This story came about for two reasons. First, it is an important prequel to my historical fiction series, *The Arthurian Age* (published by Perseid Press). That series tells the story of the Britons and their historical leader who spawned the legends of King Arthur, and their struggles against the Anglo-Saxons. It is based largely on the research of the eminent historian Geoffrey Ashe.

The second reason is that I am a major J. R. R. Tolkien nerd. When I discovered his research treatise, *Finn and Hengest* (edited by Prof. Alan Bliss), I was shocked that no one had yet published a historical fiction novel based on his thesis.

Many people are familiar with the Anglo-Saxon epic *Beowulf*. It's a pagan era poem about legendary events and people in Scandinavia and Denmark.

Fewer people have heard of the *Finnsburg Fragment*, a piece of a lost poem that describes a battle in the hall of a Frisian king named Finn.

Both poems mention a leader named Hengist, and both clearly speak of the same person and events.

Especially fascinating is that there is a significant Hengist in British history and legend. In their ancient records, the Britons and the Anglo-Saxons both describe a Hengist coming to Britain with his brother Horsa in the early fifth century. This Hengist fought for, then against the Britons and founded the first Anglo-Saxon kingdom.

Tolkien asserted that these all refer to the same Hengist, and are historical events that evolved into folklore legends.

Academics are notoriously reticent about the speculation

required to fill in the gaps in their historical research; especially when the subject matter strays into the realm of legend.

But as a historical fiction writer, I must speculate in order to fill those gaps and to find the potential links between history and legend. My only constraints are that it must be plausible and must not alter what we know of history. Whenever possible, I use the details and translated words from the original sources.

My hope is to write an enjoyable story that allows readers to immerse in the past and be able to see it clearly in their mind's eye, even if they know nothing of the era. I also hope to intrigue the people who do know something of the history. I'm amazed at how often these tales, often considered pure fiction, may be found to have their origin in history.

This story is based on the details and clues from those texts, with the insight provided by Professors Tolkien and Bliss. In writing the story, I found some surprising clues that link the history and the legends. I won't bore you with the details here, but I will soon write a blog post about it. If interested, you'll find it on my website at seanpoage.com.

Glossary, Terms and Locations

Angeln • The Angeln was the portion of modern Germany on the peninsula below Denmark. In antiquity, it would have been the tribal region of the Angles, with the Jutes to the north and the Saxons to the south.

Anglii • The Angles are one of the three main Germanic tribes that settled in Britain, along with the Saxons and Jutes. It is they who gave their name to England. It was reported that so many Angles migrated to Britain that the Angeln was left empty and abandoned.

Bononia • The late-Roman name for the modern town of Boulogne-sur-Mer. Lying on the French coast between Normandy and Calais, it was the main port for Rome's connection between Britain and the continent.

Ceorl • In early Germanic society, a ceorl was the lowest rank of free men and were primarily of the agricultural class.

Danes • The Danes were a Scandinavian Germanic tribe that originated in southern Sweden, expanding into the islands to the south and eventually into the Jutland peninsula, to which they gave their name to the country of Denmark. In the 5th century AD, they were little known to the Romans and appear to have just begun expanding into Jutland.

East Sea • The Baltic Sea.

Fates • In Germanic society, the concept of fate was a primary belief system. This was often personified in a number of female deities thought to decide the future of each human at birth. There were three chief fates, known in the later Norse period as the Norns.

Finnsburg • The site of the "Battle of Finnsburg" or the "Frisian Slaughter" as Tolkien translated. A "burg" was a fortified settlement, so this was likely Finn's primary home base. The location is unknown, the only clues being that it was in Frisia and had easy access to the sea. It may have been on one of the small islands that trace the coast of modern Netherlands or northern Germany.

Franks • The Franks were a Germanic tribal group inhabiting the region of northwestern Germany. Some settled in Britain along with the Angles, Saxons and Jutes, but for the most part, they expanded into Gaul as the Roman Empire gave way and as they defeated the Visigoths. They would give their name to France.

Frisia • Frisia was a Germanic tribal region that was roughly in the coastal area of the modern Netherlands and northwestern Germany. The Saxons and Angles would have been to their north, and the Franks to their south. They also settled Britain during the Migration Period, along with the Angles, Saxons and Jutes, but not in large enough numbers to stand out.

Fyrd • The fyrd in early Germanic society was a sort of infantry militia of freemen, typically common villagers and farmers, who were called up to supplement the ruler's core of experienced soldiers in the event of raids or war. The mobilizations were normally of short duration and the members were expected to supply their own weapons, armour and provisions.

Gaul • The name for the region of Europe composed today of France, Luxembourg, most of Switzerland, Northern Italy and parts of the Netherlands and Germany.

Geat • The Geats were a Scandinavian Germanic tribe from southern Sweden, to the north of the Danes. Beowulf, the hero from the poem *Beowulf*, was a Geat.

Germania • The Roman name for parts of north-western Europe composed today of parts of the Netherlands, Belgium, western and south-western Germany, Switzerland and eastern France.

Hearth Troops • In antiquity through the early medieval period, a warlord in Germanic and Celtic societies maintained a small retinue of full time soldiers. Warriors and warlord were bound together with oaths in an arrangement the Romans called the comitatus. These picked warriors were essentially members of the ruler's household and "shared his hearth", living in the hall with their lord.

Hildeleoma • The name of Hnaef's sword, which meant "Light of Battle".

Hispania • The Roman name for the Iberian Peninsula, now composed of Spain and Portugal.

Juteland • Now called Jutland, it is the northern three-quarters of the peninsula that makes up modern day Denmark. It was the home of the Jutes until the Danes overtook the region and gave the country its modern name.

Jutes • The Jutes were one of the three main Germanic tribes that settled in Britain, along with the Angles and Saxons. It appears that they came under the domination of the Angles for a period of time.

Rutubi • Late-Roman name for the Saxon Shore fort near Richborough in Kent.

Saxons • The Saxons were one of the three main Germanic tribes that settled in Britain, along with the Angles and Jutes. They seem to have taken their name from a large, single edged knife called a seax that was commonly carried by warriors. They lived in northwestern Germany between the Angles and the Frisians. They were such prolific raiders that the Celtic Britons called nearly anyone from Germania a "Saxon".

Scandia • Scandinavia, not including Denmark.

Scop • Scop was the Germanic term for their poets, much like the Celtic Bard.

Scythia • Scythia was the land of the Scythians: Bronze-Age nomads famed for their equestrian skills. They lived north and west of the Black Sea in modern Ukraine and southern Russia. It was considered so distant by the people of western Europe that it was a byword for the edge of the world. By the third century, AD, the Scythians had disappeared, absorbed into other cultures, but their reputation remained so that any of the nomadic horse-cultures of the steppes were often called Scythians. Finn's reference in this story is to the Huns, who were driving westward through Europe at this time.

Secgan • An unknown tribe, thought to be of the Saxons.

Tanet • Early Celtic name for the Isle of Thanet, Kent. Thanet is no longer an island, the channel having silted up over the centuries. It is said to be where Hengist and Horsa first landed in Britain.

Thegn • Thegns, (pronounced "thanes"), were the military household members of a Germanic ruler. They are typically lower-level aristocrats, often landless.

Yule • An ancient Germanic winter holiday lasting twelve days and commemorating the Winter Solstice and return of longer days. It would eventually be reinterpreted into the Christmas season holidays. Many of the Yule traditions are part of the modern celebration of Christmas, such as holly, mistletoe, evergreen trees, and carolling.

People and Characters

There are only five minor characters that I invented for this story. The rest come from the texts of *Beowulf*, the *Finnsburg Fragment*, the *Historia Brittonum*, and other historical and legendary sources listed below.

Amloth • Amloth is the ancestor of Garulf and a ruler of the Jutes who is killed by the king of the Angles. In legend and probably in history, he is called "Amlethus", is misidentified (according to Tolkien) as a Dane, and his story is placed later in history. Shakespeare uses Amleth's story as the inspiration for *Hamlet*. I follow Tolkien's speculation as the catalyst for the conflict that erupts between Garulf and Hengist.

Ceretic • In this story, Ceretic is a British merchant who speaks Germanic. He is mentioned in the 9th Century *Historia Brittonum* (History of the Britons) as Hengist's interpreter. Ceretic is a Celtic name, so it is almost certain he was a Briton.

Ceolmund • One of the five characters I invented for this story, he is one of Hengist's men.

Eadwig • One of the five characters I invented for this story, he is one of Hengist's men.

Eaha • In this story, Eaha is Hengist's closest friend and second in command. Eaha is Old English for "Warhorse", and is a nickname rather than his actual name, Octha. In history and legend, the only reference to Eaha is one brief mention in the *Finnsburg Fragment*, which describes Eaha and Sigeferth defending the door to the hall. In researching this story, I've found a fascinating possibility related to the historical Hengist. I've placed hints within this story, and more will come in *Three Wicked Revelations*, the third book in *The Arthurian Age* series, and in a future blog post.

Ealdræd • One of the five characters I invented for this story, he is one of Hengist's men. He demonstrates the Germanic style of poetry that relies on alliteration rather than rhyming.

Finn • Finn Folcwalding (son of Folcwalda) is a powerful king of Frisia. Perhaps the most powerful. At this time, it is unlikely that one "king" controlled all of any particular tribal region. He is one of the subjects of a poem that is referred to in *Beowulf*, as well as the *Finnsburg Fragment*. He also appears in an early Anglo-Saxon poem called *Widsith*, as well as the *Historia Brittonum* and some Anglo-Saxon pedigrees with different family details. He is thought to have been a historical person.

Frithuwulf • Son of Finn Folcwalding, he is only mentioned in *Beowulf*, and not by name. Tolkien's analysis of other texts led him to believe that Frithuwulf was the son most likely to have perished.

Garulf • Son of Guthulf, he is apparently the instigator of the battle at Finnsburg, leading the attack on the hall, and first to die. He is only named in the *Finnsburg Fragment*, where his father is called Guthlaf. Tolkien said this was likely a scribal error.

Guthlaf • Younger brother of Ordlaf. A Dane, he was a kinsman, probably a cousin, to Hnæf. He appears in *Beowulf* and the *Finnsburg Fragment*. Tolkien suggested that their father was Hunlaf, because of a reference to Hunlafing that implies "son (or descendant) of Hunlaf". The apparent leadership of Ordlaf and Guthlaf among the Danes suggests it was Ordlaf who placed Hnæf's sword on Hengist's lap.

Hengist • Son of Wihtgils, son of Witta, son of Wecta, son of Woden. Hengist is the protagonist behind this story, which is based on Tolkien's thesis that the Hengist of the *Historia Brittonum*, *Beowulf*, and the *Finnsburg Fragment*, are all the same historical person. He features in these and several other sources. Originally thought to be a Jute, there is evidence he was actually an Angle. Puzzlingly, his son or grandson is considered the founder of the Kentish royal dynasty, rather than himself. This story and *Three Wicked Revelations* explores possible reasons for this.

Hildeburh • Daughter of Hoc, sister of Hnæf, wife of Finn, and mother of Frithuwulf. She appears in *Beowulf*. She is a "peace-weaver", the daughter of one royal household married to another in order to cement friendly relations.

Hnæf • Son of Hoc, brother of Hildeburh, he leads the contingent that is attacked in Finn's hall and is killed, sparking the vengeance of which Hengist plays a part. He appears in *Beowulf*, the *Finnsburg Fragment* and *Widsith*.

Hoc • Father of Hnæf, his descendants would be called Hocings. He is mentioned in *Beowulf* and *Widsith*. Stories of Hoc and Hnæf were so widespread that they were included in aristocratic genealogies for centuries.

Horsa • Horsa appears in the *Historia Brittonum*, Bede's writings and the *Anglo-Saxon Chronicles*, along with his brother, Hengist. They are said to have arrived together at the Isle of Thanet in Kent, beginning the process of the Anglo-Saxon takeover of Britain. Horsa means "horse", and some claim that these references to animals show that Hengist and Horsa are mythological. However, Tolkien, the foremost Anglo-Saxon scholar, pointed out that animal names were not unknown in Germanic society.

Hrothgar • Hrothgar is recorded in *Beowulf* and *Widsith*, as well as other Anglo-Saxon and Scandinavian legends. He is likely, originally, a historical person. It is his hall that is terrorized by the monster Grendel, who Beowulf comes to kill. In this story, Hrothgar shows up near the end with Ordlaf and Guthlaf. It provides an explanation for why the Finnsburg incident is recorded within *Beowulf*.

Leofstan • One of the five characters I invented for this story, he is one of Finn's ranking soldiers.

Octha • In this story, Octha is Eaha's true name. In history and legend, Octha was either the son or grandson of Hengist. I have used this story to lay the groundwork for a possible reconciliation to be revealed in *Three Wicked Revelations*.

Oeric • In this story, Oeric is Eaha's young son. In history and legend, there is an Aesc who was born Oeric, who is said to be Hengist's son. Variations in the genealogy of Hengist and his descendants result in some confusion. My approach in this story sets the stage for explaining these discrepancies in *Three Wicked Revelations*.

Ordlaf • Elder brother to Guthlaf. A Dane, he was a kinsman, probably a cousin, to Hnæf. He appears in *Beowulf* and the *Finnsburg Fragment*. Tolkien suggested that their father was Hunlaf, because of a reference to Hunlafing that means "son (or descendant) of Hunlaf". The apparent leadership of Ordlaf and Guthlaf among the Danes suggests it was Ordlaf who placed Hnæf's sword on Hengist's lap.

Rothwen • Rothwen is the daughter of Hengist. She is referred to, but unnamed, in the *Historia Brittonum*, and called Rowena by Geoffrey of Monmouth in *The History of the Kings of Britain*. In the *Welsh Triads*, she is known as Rhonwen, and called the "Mother of the English Nation" with little affection. She will play an important role in *Three Wicked Revelations*.

Sæwine • One of the five characters I invented for this story, Sæwine is an old carpenter who helps Hengist build his ship as a youth.

Sigeferth • In this story, Sigeferth is one of Hengist's warriors. He appears in the *Widsith*, and in the *Finnsburg Fragment*, proclaiming his valour and defending the door with Eaha.

Vortigern • Vortigern is said to be the first ruler of Britain after the Britons became independent. His name is from the Brittonic for "Overlord". Some believe that it was his actual name, while others suggest it was a title, or a new name adopted upon rising to that position. The sources suggest he was not king of all Britons, but leader of a group of British rulers that came together for mutual defense against the barbarian raids that Britain suffered under. He is blamed for hiring Hengist and beginning the process that would lead to the Anglo-Saxons dominating Britain. This is explored in my upcoming novel, *Three Wicked Revelations*.

Wihtlæg • Wihtlæg was a king of the Angles said to be descended, like most Germanic royalty, from Woden. Tolkien suggested that Wihtlæg was the slayer of the Jutish ruler, Amloth, and that this was the source of conflict between Garulf and Hengist portrayed in this story. Hengist also claimed descent from Woden, but Wihtlæg does not appear as a name in his genealogy, so I have theorized that Wihtlæg was kin, perhaps brother, to Wecta, who is in Hengist's claimed genealogy.

Woden • Woden was one of the principal gods of Germanic paganism. He is known as Odin in the Viking era, which is the source of most surviving information about him. Woden was thought to preside over the hall where the souls of warriors slain in battle would go to feast. Woden is frequently claimed as an ancestor of royal houses (including Hengist's), and may have originated as a deified historical ancestor. Wednesday is named for Woden's Day.

Sources

Prof. Tolkien's translations and theories, with Prof. Bliss' input, are the basis for *Hengist*. I discovered this story primarily through the research for my Arthurian historical fiction series, *The Arthurian Age*. Much of the material for that series applies to this story. Below is a small selection of the sources I use. For more, visit my website and blog at seanpoage.com.

Alcock, Leslie. *Economy, Society, and Warfare Among the Britons and Saxons C400-C800 A.D.* University of Wales Press, 1987.

Bede. *The Ecclesiastical History of the English People.* Oxford University Press, UK, 1999.

Bromwich, Rachel. *Trioedd Ynys Prydein: The Triads of the Island of Britain.* University of Wales Press, 2014.

Geoffrey of Monmouth. *The History of the Kings of Britain.* Translated by Lewis Thorpe, Penguin Books, 2004.

Halsall, Guy. *Warfare and Society in the Barbarian West.* Routledge, 2005.

Haywood, John. *Dark Age Naval Power: A Reassessment of Frankish and Anglo-Saxon Seafaring Activity.* Anglo-Saxon Books, 2006.

Laycock, Stuart. Warlords: *The Struggle for Power in Post-Roman Britain*. The History Press, 2009.

Nennius. *Historia Brittonum: The History of the Britons*. Kessinger Publishing, LLC, 2010.

Tacitus. *The Agricola and The Germania*. Translated by Harold B. Mattingly and J. B. Rives, Penguin, 2010.

Tolkien, J. R. R. *Beowulf: A Translation and Commentary*, Together with Sellic Spell. Edited by Christopher Tolkien, HarperCollins Publishers, 2016.

Tolkien, J. R. R. *Finn and Hengest: The Fragment and the Episode*. Edited by Alan Bliss, Harper Collins, 2006.

Yale Law School, The Avalon Project, "The Anglo-Saxon Chronicle : Fifth Century"
https://avalon.law.yale.edu/medieval/ang05.asp

Meet Sean Poage

Sean has had an exciting and varied life as a laborer, salesman, soldier, police officer, investigator, computer geek and author. A history buff since childhood, he is most drawn to the eras of the ancient Greeks and Dark Ages Britain. Traveling the world to see history up close is his passion.

These days he works in the tech world, writes when he can, and spends the rest of his time with his family and house full of furballs, which usually means chores and home improvement projects. When the stars align, he finds time for a scuba dive or hike in the beautiful Maine outdoors. Check out his blog on seanpoage.com.

Fifteen hundred years have turned history into legend…

Decades after independence from Rome, Britain has finally clawed its way back to peace and prosperity. Across the sea, Rome crumbles under barbarian attacks, internal corruption and civil war. Desperate for allies, Rome's last great emperor looks to Britain and the rising fame of her High King, Arthur.

Gawain, a young warrior craving fame, is swept up in Arthur's wake. While his family faces their own struggles at home, Gawain finds himself taking on more than he bargained for, marching into a terrible war far from home.

The Retreat to Avalon, published by Perseid Press, is the exciting beginning of the historical fiction trilogy *The Arthurian Age*, introducing readers to the origins of King Arthur and the world he lived and fought for.

Enjoy this sneak peek at *Three Wicked Revelations,* picking up where *Hengist* leaves off…

Chapter One
428 A.D.

Vortigern surveyed the main room of the once grand praetorium with disgust. Water dripped where rain found its way through sparse thatch piled over broken roof tiles that should have been removed long ago. Mould stained the peeling plaster of the walls and assaulted his nose. The floor was so scuffed and worn that he could not even identify the theme portrayed by the cracked mosaic tiles.

He spun on his heel and headed for the door, scattering servants and sycophants from his path. "Prepare my pavilion. This is unfit for human habitation."

He strode through the rubbish-filled courtyard and out of the building. Slaves rushed to raise a leathern sheet over his gaunt frame to deflect the rain from his rich robes and carefully coiffed, black hair. He crossed his arms and gazed around the wide parade field. It had been many years since any troops marched there. Not since Constantine had stripped Britain's garrisons and departed for Rome, some twenty years past.

He shook his head. Rutubi had been Rome's gateway to Britain. A tremendous marble and gold arch a hundred feet tall once stood here among gleaming stone buildings.

Now the place stank of urine, dung, and sulphur. The locals penned their animals in the old fort at night. The barracks and other buildings would probably need to be torn down and rebuilt. Only a wooden church and a few monks' huts in the northwest corner were properly maintained.

The monks huddled nearby, nervously watching him and the ranks of soldiers standing like statues in the rain.

"Summon the abbot," Vortigern said without looking over his shoulder.

One of his attendants scurried over to the monks, and returned with an aged man in tattered brown robes.

"My lord," the old monk croaked, bowing. "How may I be of service?"

"Where is the commander of this fort? Where is the garrison?"

"My lord, the garrison dissolved years ago. As they went unpaid, they took to farming, or left. The descendants of those who stayed bring their families here and man the walls when the heathens come, but they have little in the way of arms or training."

Vortigern tapped a finger on his arm, scowling. This was the fifth Saxon Shore fortress he had inspected, and the last two were in similar states. Those further north were reportedly no better. *Where will I find the troops to refortify them?*

A distant horn blast interrupted his thoughts. It repeated several times: quick, strident bleats. More horns answered from other directions, joined by the clank of metal on metal.

"Heathens!" the abbot cried out, pale and wide-eyed.

"Where?" Vortigern's head snapped towards the open gate, then to his soldiers, whose trepidation was evident in their shifting stances and darting eyes. "Get men on the walls! Secure the gate!" *Picts or Saxons? How close are they?*

As most of the soldiers rushed for the gate or the stairs leading to the rampart, the old abbot clasped his hands and nearly fell to his knees. "Lord, the people? Your subjects!

They will come here for safety. We must keep the gate open for them!"

"We? Are you responsible for this fortress? If so, you have much to answer for." Vortigern turned and marched off towards the eastern wall, a remaining file of ten soldiers jogging to catch up. "Once this disturbance is resolved."

The east gate, like those on the north and south walls, was closed and blocked up with timbers and rubble. Two of Vortigern's men stopped the rest from following him up the crumbling steps to the top of the wall. The rest followed him, pausing as Vortigern hesitated at the last step.

There was no sign of a hostile force. Below the walls, the high tide lapped at the old wharf. He saw no ships, and the Isle of Tanet, scarcely a stade off, was obscured by the rain.

He looked back to see the western gate was shut and his men had pushed wagons up against it. Other soldiers stood watch on the north and south walls, but none appeared to have sighted any enemy.

With a grunt of irritation, Vortigern picked his way back down the stairs and through the mob of servants, functionaries, and minions that dogged his every step. He knew that the look on his face would discourage anyone from speaking up.

If Veranconus wasn't such an incompetent, I would not have been caught in this glorified swine pen.

The captain of his guard was inspecting the barricade at the gate, and a few of his soldiers stood on the parapet above, looking out over the battlements. As he approached, he heard a clamour of shouts and wailing from outside the gate. His knees weakened with dread.

"The enemy is at the gates?" he called out as he approached.

The captain turned and went rigid. "No, lord. Those are

the citizens, begging for entry."

Vortigern grimaced, glanced back up at the battlements. "Why are your men on the wall instead of the tower, where they can see further?"

"The wooden floors in the towers are rotting and unstable, lord."

One man, rotund with protruding front teeth detached from the cluster of people following Vortigern and approached, bowing. Vortigern pretended not to notice.

"Lord, it seems no enemy is near enough to threaten the gates," the man lisped. "Might we open them long enough to allow the people in?"

"The magistrate of Cantia is responsible for four of the Saxon Shore forts. Do you understand their purpose, Veranconus?"

"Er . . . yes, my lord. Defence against barbarian raiders."

Vortigern turned and looked down his long, narrow nose at Veranconus. "Their purpose is to project power. To deter barbarians from even considering Britain's coast. Considering the condition of the forts in your charge, is it any surprise the enemy does not hesitate to land at will?"

"Lord, Cantia has borne the brunt of barbarian attacks for a century. Half our citizenry has fled west, or across the sea to Letavia. I've had to concentrate our meagre resources at Regulv to guard the mouth of the Tamesis and protect Lundein."

"Bah." Vortigern looked back at the gate. The clamour outside continued. *Always excuses with these bureaucrats. Yet never are their own estates unguarded, or their tables bare.*

"Lord, the people?" Veranconus whined. "If we bring them in, we will have more defenders, as well as their animals to withstand a siege."

"Of course I will let them in," Vortigern snapped. He waved to his captain, who jogged over. "If there is no sign of the enemy, open the gate enough to allow the people to file in, but be prepared to close it if the enemy is sighted." As the soldier turned to follow the order, Vortigern added, "And find whoever raised the alarm."

A nagging pain grew behind his eyes. He turned and went to his pavilion, just erected on the parade field, and told his guards to admit none but his servants, or their captain with important news. The servants rushed to bring his furniture from the wagons and put everything in its place while he glowered impatiently.

He sagged into a chair and called for wine and a damp rag to cover his eyes. Perhaps he had been mad to accept this role as leader of the Consilium. The idea for the council had been his, of course. It was the only way to unite the aristocracy to face Britain's external threats, and mitigate the internal strife that persisted in the eighteen years since Britain revolted from Rome.

Perhaps his madness lay in believing the flatterers who convinced him to lead the council. Friends come in times of fortune and depart in times of adversity, but enemies tend to accumulate in both cases.

His achievements inspired the usual jealousies, particularly from those yearning for the return of the Roman yoke. That faction, led by those insufferable Ambrosii, relentlessly attacked him, as if he should have been able to end the barbarian raids and restore the Roman trade in the little more than two years of his reign.

They sought to discredit him, sending a grovelling letter to the Romans, begging for their return and protection. The Roman rebuttal gave Vortigern no small amount of pleasure, but the pressure for some evidence of progress had finally pushed him to this long, miserable slog from one dilapidated fortress to the next. He could no longer leave it to the magistrates and their intermediaries. He would learn what was true and what was ineptitude, and he would make changes.

He almost longed for the simpler days of his youth, when Britain was Roman, and he was called Vitalinus.

A scuffing of feet and a soft cough from the tent's entrance announced the end of his respite. Vortigern removed the cloth and turned his head to see his captain waiting.

"News of the Saxons?" Vortigern asked.

"Lord, fishermen sighted three Saxon warships landing on Tanet, two miles north of here. They raised the alarm."

Three ships. An army that outnumbers my guard. "So, a hundred, maybe two hundred pirates. Have they left yet? What damage?"

"Lord . . . They set a camp, and none have ventured beyond it."

"Not raiding?" Vortigern stared at him, puzzled. "What are they doing?"

"I know not, lord. They just sit there. They blew a horn and killed a calf, then hung the calf's head on a tent."

"What is that about? Are they plague bearers?"

"There's no telling, lord. There are a thousand Saxon tribes, and each keeps its own customs."

"Reconnoitre their camp. If peaceful and not diseased, send an envoy."

*

Hours later, Vortigern stood on the battlement above the wharf. The rain had ceased and the setting sun's last rays peered beneath the clouds to warm his back. A small boat approached, crowded with his soldiers and a dozen of the Saxon warriors. They were still too far out for details, but the Saxons stood a head taller than his own men, and their varied and brightly coloured clothing contrasted with his own soldier's drab blue cloaks.

One of the Saxons looked up at the ramparts, directly, Vortigern thought, at him. His breath caught, and he stepped back from the parapet. He looked around at the few guards standing nearby, their faces blank. Behind him, and below, the sycophants waited, their faces raised expectantly. He turned and strode down the stairs, glad that the east gate was blocked up. It would take some time for the visitors to go around to the west gate.

His scouts had found a simple camp of about one hundred and fifty men. The Saxons were wary, but showed no sign of disease or ill-intent. A local Briton named Ceretic, a former merchant who spoke the Saxon language, offered to parley with the strangers. The result was this imminent meeting. Vortigern returned to his tent to inspect the preparations. Whatever these Saxons wanted, he intended to impress them.

He took his seat on the throne beneath his pavilion's awning. His right hand rested on the sheathed sword across his knees, and he held a stem of holly in his left. His crowd of followers, carefully arranged to either side behind him, spilled out from under the cover of the oiled linen tarp.

All was in order when the delegation passed the west gate. Vortigern's soldiers, cleaned and polished, flanked the path from the gate to his pavilion. The Saxons made an impressive entrance in their proud march behind Vortigern's captain, but the graceful strides of the leading pair of Saxons made everyone around them look clumsy. Tall and imposing, with dusky hair and drooping moustaches under long, straight noses, their features were so alike that Vortigern was certain they were brothers separated by a few years.

His captain stopped the procession at the rugs before the tent so that slaves could scurry forward to wash the mud from the visitors' shoes. He then directed the first two Saxons to step forward, followed by Ceretic.

"Welcome, strangers," Vortigern opened, raising the sprig of holly. "Who are you, from where do you come, and why have you brought so many warlike men to these shores?"

Ceretic murmured to the man on the left, whose hair was knotted atop his head and appeared to be the elder. The man took a half-step forward and bowed, his arms sweeping out to his sides, and replied in the harsh Saxon tongue to Vortigern.

"Lord, we are of the Iutae," Ceretic translated. "I am Hengist, son of Wictgils, son of Witta, sons of heroes in long descent from Woden, All-Father." Hengist held up a carved ivory idol that hung by a thong around his neck, then motioned to the man beside him. "This is my brother, Horsa. We come in search of a worthy prince to serve, for it is a custom of our people, when our country has become over-populated, to choose young men by lot to leave and seek their fortunes in other lands."

"Glad am I to find you peacefully upon our shores," Vortigern replied. "While I grieve that such noble men are not followers of the True Faith, it may be that our Holy Father, whose designs are beyond mortal ken, has brought you hither, not for our benefit alone, but for your souls, as well."

"You have the tongue of a true king." Hengist smiled. "We, renowned warriors with no skill at tilling the earth, find ourselves in need of a patron as the first golden leaves herald winter's approach. There may be no doubt that Fate has guided us here, to the wise Overlord of Britannia, whose troubles with the Picts are known even in our country." He took a step forward and went to one knee. "Let us serve you and bring an end to their depredations."

Vortigern regarded Hengist and Horsa gravely, his finger tapping the sheath of his sword. *Heaven shows me favour, yet again. The Consilium will demand a vote to approve a long-term agreement, but Rome has long hired mercenaries for border protection. These Sax—or rather, Yoo-teh, as they call themselves—may be the answer to our dilemma.* He nodded, and said, "It is true that we are beset on all sides, no less by attacks from Germania. If you and your men take service to defend our shores, will you defend against any, even your own kinsmen?"

"I cannot speak for other tribes, but you need not fear our kin while we are in your service, and we will drive off any who threaten your shores."

"I must consult my councillors before a final decision is made." Vortigern stood, handing his sword to a youth behind his chair. "Until such a time, you and your men may remain on the isle where your ships now rest. In exchange for your service during this time, you will receive food, clothing and shelter befitting trusted warriors."

He stepped down from the dais, took Hengist's hand and raised him to stand. "And now as guests, join me for food and drink, and tell me all about your people and your history."

* * *

Learn more at seanpoage.com

www.ingramcontent.com/pod-product-compliance
Lightning Source LLC
Chambersburg PA
CBHW020047310726
48970CB00007B/2446